Why Women Earn Le$$

How to Make What You're *Really* Worth

By

Mikelann R. Valterra

FOREWORD BY BARBARA STANNY

CAREER
PRESS
Franklin Lakes, NJ

WHY WOMEN EARN LESS
EDITED BY KATHRYN HENCHES
TYPESET BY EILEEN DOW MUNSON
Cover design by Lu Rossman/Digi Dog Design
Printed in the U.S.A. by Book-mart Press

To order this title, please call toll-free 1-800-CAREER-1 (NJ and Canada: 201-848-0310) to order using VISA or MasterCard, or for further information on books from Career Press.

The Career Press, Inc., 3 Tice Road, PO Box 687,
Franklin Lakes, NJ 07417
www.careerpress.com

Library of Congress Cataloging-in-Publication Data

Valterra, Mikelann R., 1969-
    Why women earn less : how to make what you're really worth / by Mikelann R. Valterra ; foreword by Barbara Stanny.
        p. cm.
    Includes bibliographical references and index.
    ISBN 1-56414-689-8 (paper)
    1. Wages—Women. 2. Women—Employment. 3. Equal pay for equal work. 4. Women—Finance, Personal. I. Title.

HD6061.V35 2004
331.4'2153—dc22

2003065535

For Karen McCall,

my mentor,

my friend,

and a true pioneer.

Acknowledgments

I am blessed to be surrounded by supportive, caring people who believed in this project from the start. My special thanks go to:

Karen McCall, who gave me the gift of this work. I often wonder where I would be in my life had I not met her. It is her years of work and thought that shine through these pages.

Elsa Hurley, my amazing agent. She fought for me, encouraged me, listened to me, and made me believe that this project would make a big difference in the lives of countless women. In addition to great advice and insightful feedback, she was a wonderful editor—a service I will be eternally grateful for.

Lorraine Howell, who pushed me to do this project, when I didn't think I was ready to do so.

Barbara Stanny, for agreeing to write the foreword and her willingness to give advice.

Vicki McCown, who edited the original proposal and saw the potential.

Candice Fuhrman, who took a chance on a young unknown author and offered her representation.

David Liatos, my CPA, who helped with numbers.

Bethany Collins, the best manuscript reader a writer could hope to find.

Raylene Gokeri, who gave great feedback and always assumed I'd write an amazing book.

Kathleen Craig, who believed in this project and has always supported me. (I love you, honey!)

Raymond Warrick, a wonderful sounding board, who offered constant support and encouragement.

My mother, Joy Barton, who is my number one fan. Upon hearing I secured a book contract, she sent me flowers with a message that read: "It's like watching a rocket taking off." There is just nothing like having a mother who believes great things are in store for you. Everything I am, I owe to her.

David Barton, my father, who told me from the time I was young that the world was my oyster. He said I could do anything, and I believed him.

Grace, my mother-in-law, who is an extraordinary woman in her own right. She helped me to truly understand the joys of voluntary simplicity coupled with financial literacy. She is a remarkable woman.

Anthony, my amazing husband. To say he is my rock does not do him justice. He read my words before anyone else saw them, checking my thoughts, my writing, and my sanity. Without him, I could not have written this book. (I love you, honey. We make a great team!)

The women in my six-week underearning class. Their honesty and willingness to go deep to find the answers, inspired me to no end. I wish every one of them high earnings!

Lastly, my financial counseling clients. For years I have been privileged to work with amazing people. In the course of doing their work and pursuing their own truth, they have taught me much. Thank you.

Author's Note

In 1996, I was lucky enough to become one of the first Financial Recovery Counselors that Karen McCall trained in her methodology of financial counseling. Many of the processes, concepts, and ideas that I learned through my work with Karen McCall and the Financial Recovery Institute are incorporated in this book. Financial Recovery Counseling teaches basic money management skills. It also examines how an individual's life experiences, and underlying attitudes and beliefs about money, help shape and drive their self-defeating patterns around money. The Institute's MoneyMinder program is a practical approach to solving a wide range of financial problems, including chronic debting, compulsive spending, underearning, and managing inherited wealth.

One of the cornerstones of Financial Recovery Counseling is working with clients on developing a personalized spending plan, and the Financial Recovery spending plan process was used as the backbone in designing the "earnings plan" in Chapter 6. You will find many of Karen McCall's concepts in these pages. To the extent that I have incorporated aspects of the Financial Recovery process and/or MoneyMinder tools herein, it is with the permission of Karen McCall and the Financial Recovery Institute, who retain all rights therein, and further use or duplication of Institute material by any other person is prohibited. You may contact the Institute at *www.financialrecovery.com*.

Table of Contents

Foreword
by Barbara Stanny

You have in your hands a groundbreaking financial book. I've spent years researching the field of women and finance, and I'm continually surprised at how little attention has been paid to underearning, even though it's an insidious phenomenon that can cost a woman hundreds of thousands of dollars over a lifetime.

Fortunately for us, Mikelann Valterra has used her years of experience as a financial counselor to shed new light on a common condition that few people talk about—even the experts—while offering concrete ways to solve the problem.

When I began researching my latest book, *Secrets of Six-Figure Women,* I noticed that discussion of women's earnings focused almost exclusively on the wage gap. It's widely known that the workplace is skewed to favor men. There is a glass ceiling. There is gender discrimination. There is an old boys' network. Women get fewer raises, smaller bonuses, and less frequent promotions than men. But what isn't widely known is that these factors are only *part* of the problem.

Despite all of the workplace and cultural challenges we women face, the surprising truth is that the real culprit isn't actually "out there" at all. I wholeheartedly agree with Mikelann

Valterra when she boldly declares, "I believe that many women are responsible for their own underearning." How? We unconsciously sabotage our success by the way we think.

To most women, the salary gap feels like an inescapable trap. A 1999 "fiscal fitness" study noted that 55 percent of women worried about money a great deal. And rightfully so. The average woman earns $10,000 less than the average man, bringing in only $27,355, according to the U.S. Census Bureau. And seven out of 10 women never retire because they can't afford to. But other than worrying and engaging in wishful thinking, what can we do? Most of us haven't a clue. Because no one ever taught us how to achieve financial success, too many of us assume we can't.

How often have you found yourself thinking, "I wish I made more money?" Only to add with a sigh, "Someday...maybe someday..."

Well, someday has arrived. Today is the day to start turning your vague desires into a deep-seated commitment. It's the day to shift from building castles in the air to laying the foundation. The book you're about to read will show you the way.

As you will learn in the pages that follow, the key to overcoming underearning is to break through our myths, outmoded beliefs, and early messages about ourselves and money. Mikelann Valterra is a pioneer, exploring new territory, offering invaluable insight you won't find anywhere else.

Reading this book is like putting your psyche under a magnifying glass. You will discover why you've been underearning, how you can change, and a step-by-step plan for making more money. This book is the closest you'll get to hand-holding with a financial counselor without having to make an appointment with one.

It's an easy read, but deserves to be savored slowly, thoughtfully. There's so much wisdom and insight to be found in these chapters. You'll want to have a yellow marker handy for highlighting, and a pen for making notes in the margin. In my opinion, the most powerful way to experience this book would be to share it with others. Chapter 9 talks about how to form a book club or study group for this purpose. One thing is for sure, as Mikelann points out, "once you start reading, you've embarked on the process."

Oh what a thrilling journey it promises to be!

—Barbara Stanny

Author of *Secrets of Six-figure Women: Surprising Strategies to Up Your Earnings and Change Your Life,* and *Prince Charming Isn't Coming: How Women Get Smart About Money.*

Introduction

Many women are not making enough money, and it is time to be honest about this. What about you? Are you making enough money? Could you make more? Are you earning at your potential? What will your own future look like? The truth is that countless women are locked in a cycle of "underearning." They consistently make less money than they need, or they continually earn below their potential, despite their experience, education, or even desire to make more money. They are frustrated, and many are afraid.

Underearning is simply the pattern of not making enough money throughout one's life. Because it does not seem as overtly harmful as debt and overspending, it has long been overlooked as the serious financial problem that it is. It is not an "in your face" financial crisis, unlike overwhelming debt or out of control finances. This, perhaps, is why this pattern has been ignored for so long. It affects women's lives even more profoundly than these other behaviors and, because it can go unnoticed for so long, its effects compound to staggering proportions.

As much as some women would like to avoid thinking about money, the reality is that they have no choice. Eighty to 90 percent of all women will be solely responsible for their own finances, at some point in their lives. This is due to the high divorce rate, which hovers between 50 and 60 percent, depending on what you read, and the shocking fact that the average age of widowhood for American women is 55. In fact, 90 percent of all American women end their lives alone, through divorce, widowhood, or never marrying. So yes, we must think about how to take care of ourselves financially; inevitably, it will be all up to us.

Overcoming underearning is about self-created financial stability. There is no substitute for the self-confidence and security that financial stability provides us. And making good money is about more than just the money. When we make "enough," when we earn at our potential, we feel capable of anything. We can follow our ambition and achieve amazing goals. Instead of being an obstacle in our lives, money becomes a blessing; it doesn't stand in our way anymore. And when we earn enough, we know deep down that we can do, or handle, anything that comes our way.

Why am I so passionate about underearning? Because in my work as a financial counselor, I have seen it first hand. I've seen the effects of long-term underearning. Women come into my office in their sixties after a lifetime of not earning enough money, and they feel as if they have few options open to them. They fear the future and regret the past. It pains me greatly to see the loss of freedom that underearning represents for so many women. But I have also seen the possibilities that open up in women's lives when underearning is conquered. Life expands and they are able to pursue opportunities. And when women start making enough money, they look forward to the future, and the comfort and security that await them.

Yet I continually marvel at the veil of secrecy and silence that surrounds underearning, despite how deeply it has permeated our culture. No one talks about the fact that so many women are not making enough money. No one talks about the chronic phenomena of always earning below our potential. We need to be honest with ourselves and tell the truth. When we shroud this issue in silence, women continue suffering financially in isolation. And this silence fuels the feelings of frustration that so many feel around money.

There is also a lot of shame that surrounds issues of money. It is as if we say to ourselves, "What is wrong with me that prevents me from figuring this out?" It is frustrating, because we know we are intelligent women. But then, why do we fall into self-defeating patterns around money? The truth is that money issues go far beyond our intellect. Money taps into our deepest emotions and symbolizes what we fear, hope for, and desire, in life. With such potent emotional baggage, is it any wonder that underearning is such a problem? Where does one even begin? How does one overcome underearning?

That is what this book is about. I want to help you understand your underearning and make more money. With this book, you will:

ⓢ Identify your own history of underearning.

ⓢ Explore what is behind your underearning.

ⓢ Learn concrete skills to increase your income.

Without being able to pinpoint your own underearning, it is very difficult to see the necessity of changing. That is what Chapter 1 explores. And discovering why you underearn is a necessary precursor to action. Without understanding what is unconsciously driving our underearning, we run the risk of changing the behavior only temporarily, and then in time, reverting back to our former self.

Chapters 2, 3, and 4 center on helping you explore why you are really underearning. These chapters focus on three questions:

1. Does a part of me believe there is virtue in not having a lot of money?

2. Am I secretly waiting for someone else to do it
    for me?

3. Is underearning in any way benefiting me?

And then it is time for action. Once you've analyzed your underearning, what do you do? You will:

- Explore the surprising relationship of debt and
  financial vagueness to underearning.

- Calculate exactly how much money you need to
  be earning.

- Heal the disconnect that exists between work and
  money.

- Learn how to negotiate for more money, be it a
  raise or salary negotiation.

By the end, you will also see many more practical steps you can take to increase your earnings. Along the way you will meet women who have struggled with underearning, and follow them as they examine their motivations and take action to bring in more money.

You will get the most out of this book by reading it slowly and taking the time to answer the journal questions and do the exercises. In this way, you will internalize the concepts and begin working on eliminating your own underearning. You will find many fascinating concepts in this book. Some will speak to you and some won't. Underearning affects women in different ways, so take what is useful to you and leave the rest.

It is my sincerest hope that this book opens you up to the possibility of making more money, and gives you the tools to do so. Many women have overcome their underearning, and you can too. What would it be like if you removed money as a barrier to your dreams? Anything would be possible. And when we earn our potential, we prove to ourselves that we are in control of our lives. There is nothing that compares to the feeling of self-confidence and self-reliance that making money provides us.

Take a moment and visualize the woman you will be in 30 years. Where does she live? What kind of life does she lead? Is she happy? Is she secure, and not worrying about her finances? How you deal with money now, and the amount of money you make now, deeply affects her. It determines the type of life she leads, and the possibilities she has. Would this future self ask you to pay more attention to money, so she could lead a fuller life, with more opportunities and more comfort? Commit now to taking care of her, and from the bottom of her heart, she will thank you. Remember, her future lies in your hands.

Chapter One

The Truth About Underearning

Sitting at her desk, the woman looked forlornly out the window at the overcast sky. The weather echoed her mood and seemed to affirm the bleak future she was envisioning. Her hand clasped her latest paycheck, which she had just examined. She just wasn't making enough money. Who was she kidding? She had never made enough. So why would things change in the future? Her stomach churned as she thought of her mounting credit card debt. How would she ever climb out? Yet she had almost gotten used to living under constant financial stress, going from one crisis to the next. She would survive. She always had.

But in her heart, she knew she wanted to make more. Images of a new car, nicer clothes, and her own home tantalized her. Yet she felt trapped. She couldn't imagine ever getting ahead at this job. But it also felt too late to move to another job. If only she had asked for more when she first started! But would it really have made a big enough difference?

Anger swelled up inside her. She had done so well with so little, for so long. But in the end, it looked like there just wouldn't be enough. She looked at the paltry amount going into her 401(k), and again, it felt like too little, too late. She could feel her fantasy of one day being a contented old woman, puttering away in her charming little cottage garden, give way to night-mare images of being an old homeless woman, wandering the streets....

The $500,000 Question

Have any of those thoughts or frustrations ever gone through your head? Would you like to earn more money? Are you tired of not making the money you suspect you should be making? Would having more money help you pay off debts and build savings? I suspect you would say yes. Countless women long to make more money, but just don't know how to go about it. They feel "stuck"—uncertain how to move ahead.

Many women chronically earn less than they could, and are tired and frustrated at their apparent inability to increase their earnings. This pattern of not making enough money is called "underearning," and is a tragic waste of potential and possibil-ity in the lives of thousands of women. Underearning happens when you repeatedly (and consistently) make less than you need or than would be helpful to you, usually despite your desire to make more money. Put another way: An underearner is some-one who doesn't get paid as much as might be expected, given her experience, education, and training.

Underearning takes on many forms and can be as creative and varied as the underearner. Those on a salary may have a hard time asking for that long overdue raise, while those who are self-employed might find it difficult to raise their fees. Some-times people give their time away by underbilling. Others underearn by using all their energy for volunteer activities, and in the process give away their skills and experience. And some people underearn by failing to market themselves, whether or not they are self-employed.

Some of these practices are part of everyday life, and are so common that most women do not understand how their behav-ior limits their earning potential. Also, underearning can result from what one *doesn't* do, which makes it more easily unnoticed, ignored, or forgotten. But the end result is the same: when women undersell themselves, the price they pay is very high.

Millions of women underearn—yet have no idea they are doing so. During the course of a working lifetime, this chronic underselling results in the loss of what most of us would consider a small fortune. In fact, current research shows that the average 25-year-old woman will earn $523,000 *less* than her male counterpart over the next 40 years, according to the Institute of Women's Policy Research. Imagine—more than half a million dollars lost, never to be recouped!

That's the bad news. The good news is that many of the causes of underearning can be eliminated, and you have the power to make that happen, though you may not yet realize it. It *is* possible to make more money. But in order to do so, you must first learn how to recognize your own underearning, and to understand the issues that motivate your behavior. Only then can you develop a solid, workable plan to reverse the pattern of selling yourself short.

But first, we must unveil underearning and shine a spotlight on it. Despite how common underearning is, no one talks about it. In fact, it is considered down right rude to discuss how much one earns. So in essence, you are not allowed to discuss one of the most important things in your life: money.

It never fails. After every talk I give or seminar I conduct on the subject of underearning, I hear the same comments over and over: "I felt as though you were speaking directly to me, like you had a window into my life." "You've named something that I've always felt but couldn't quite put my finger on." "Finally, I know what's stopping me from achieving the financial success that I want."

As I said in the Introduction, I continually marvel at the veil of secrecy and silence that surrounds underearning. Somehow underearning has escaped detection by financial experts, failed to excite the media, and never found a forum for public discussion. Perhaps it stems from our reticence to discuss money issues in public. In this age of full disclosure and talk shows that reveal our most intimate secrets, talking about money has survived as the last great cultural taboo. As a result, many money problems fester in secret. And when it is hard to talk about something with other people, it's also hard to face it ourselves.

I often hear women express concern about their economic futures. They wonder whether they will be able to afford housing, food, and medical care in their later years. Many are afraid that, once they retire, they will have to depend on relatives or government aid to get along. In some cases, this uncertainty can cause extreme anxiety; in fact, I've listened to more than one of my clients express her fear of becoming a bag lady, poor and homeless, destined to endlessly wander the streets asking for handouts to survive. We will explore this idea and fear of being a bag lady in Chapter 3.

Even if this bag lady scenario seems a bit farfetched, it symbolizes a deep and predominant sense of economic insecurity in women—an insecurity that, unfortunately, is firmly rooted in reality. According to the Social Security Administration, more than 13 percent of elderly women live below the poverty line—almost twice that of men. And if we look at single elderly women (who are divorced, widowed, or never married), the poverty rate is 19 percent. That's almost one in five! And countless more simply do not have enough money to live life as fully as they would wish.

Underearning affects us both now and in the future. When we underearn, we have less money to enjoy life, cover our necessities and save for the future. Not earning enough money, and hence not having enough money, prevents us from taking advantage of many opportunities. And of course, not having enough money leads to a host of stressful financial situations, from not having enough to pay the bills, to running up credit card debt.

And underearning will affect us deeply in the future. If you have spent a lifetime underearning, you will have less money when your earning years are over. Whether it's social security compensation, IRAs, or 401(k)s you have paid into, the bottom-line balance in any retirement plan will be significantly lessened by the fact that you earned less than you could have throughout your working life. Because of this, it is not unusual for a retired woman to find that her monthly income just isn't enough to cover her needs. And although we may be tempted to think there will be someone there to care for us, statistically, this just isn't true. Eighty to 90 percent of American women, at one time or another in their lives, become wholly responsible for their economic welfare. (This is because nine out of 10 American women end up alone—single, divorced, or widowed.)

Whether you are single or married, taking economic responsibility is an absolute necessity. And if you choose to temporarily leave the work force to raise a family, you may face an especially difficult challenge, for you must compensate for those years of lost earnings. When the effects of underearning are added to this loss of income, the results can be devastating. If you choose to stay home for a time, fulfilling your earning potential during the years you do bring home a paycheck plays an important role in your retirement years.

Moving up the Continuum

Just about everyone has failed to realize their earning potential at some point during their working years. This is not underearning. We all suffer occasional financial setbacks due to a lost job, a career switch, a need to focus on family issues, and the like. These are temporary events—part of the ebb and flow of life. Underearning, on the other hand, follows a pattern of repeated behavior that brings about the same outcome over and over again. It can be easy to see each event in isolation. Each time you underearn may look reasonable in and of itself, pegged to a certain event or decision. But when you step back, you must ask yourself: *Is there a pattern of self-defeating behavior?*

When I speak on underearning, I tell my audiences to visualize a continuum labeled "Earning Potential." At one end of the earning scale they will find those people who never seem to underearn. They consistently land the right job and get paid the large salaries.

In the middle of the continuum are what I call "problematic" underearners. While underearning may not wreak havoc in their lives, they have underearned enough times, and in enough ways, that to stop doing so would greatly enhance their financial worth.

At the other end of the scale are the compulsive underearners. These people are locked into a pattern of underearning they feel powerless to break. Despite the negative consequences they suffer, despite the fact that they may want to stop, they cannot. They are doomed to repeat this destructive behavior throughout their working lives unless they are willing to look at its causes and commit to making the concrete changes that will allow them to create a new, healthier, more profitable pattern.

Active vs. Passive Underearning

Underearning is difficult to spot because sometimes it is about what we are doing, and at other times, it is about what we are *not* doing. Jerrold Mundis, author of the 1995 book *Earn What You Deserve* (Bantam, 1996), makes the point that underearning may be "active" or "passive," and he categorizes examples of underearning as one or the other. Passive underearning is defined as not doing, or failing to do something that would—if you had done it—cause you to earn more, such as not asking for a raise. Not capitalizing on your skills or taking advantage of opportunities are also examples of passive underearning. So is failing to create a career plan. Active underearning, on the other hand, involves doing something that results in underearning—such as quitting a job, setting low fees, and turning work down. Active underearning also occurs when you spend time on activities that make little or no money, or when you accept work that you know will pay you less than you need.

Obviously, active underearning can be easier to spot, but both active and passive underearning are detrimental to our earnings ability. And passive underearning is one reason why underearning can feel so insidious, because underearning is so frequently about what we don't do. There may be no behavior that sticks out to us as self-defeating. Rather, it is our inaction that can be self-defeating.

It's All Relative

When they are first introduced to the concept of underearning, many people often mistake it for underachieving. But this is not correct, for underearners can achieve great things and still not be adequately compensated for their work. Another misconception is that underearners simply do not work enough; again, the opposite it more likely to be true. Underearners typically are intelligent, hard-working people. In fact, many are workaholics who put in long hours at the office, trying to get ahead. Yet, despite their dedication, the pay they receive is not commensurate with the time and effort that they put forth.

One key to identifying true underearning is to understand that it is a relative concept. What may well be underearning for one person is not for another. All that matters is whether you are making enough money for *you*. For example, consider the woman who lives in a mid-sized town and runs a small deli, bringing home about $40,000 a year. Her life is comfortable, her family's needs and wants are provided for, and she consistently contributes to her savings. Now compare the earning habits of another woman, a self-employed business consultant who lives in a metropolitan area. Even though she takes in over $85,000 a year, her business expenses and lifestyle consume most of her income, and she lives from paycheck to paycheck, as she has for much of her adult life.

Which Woman is the Underearner?

Clearly, underearning cannot be defined in absolutes. It is not measured by how much money one earns or how high a position one holds, but by whether that person's needs and wants are being met. And for the chronic underearner, their wants and needs are seldom being met. The truth is that underearners seem to subconsciously find a way for the world *not* to pay them enough.

It's important to note that overcoming underearning is not about simply trying to make as much money as humanly possible. In fact, those people who are driven to make as much money as they can, no matter what, may suffer from "compulsive overearning," in itself an unhealthy pattern of behavior. Rather, women must learn how to recognize the patterns that keep them from earning what they need, remove those causes, and thereby unlock their earning potential.

A crucial first step is to ask yourself whether you are falling into an unconscious pattern, or are making conscious choices. For example, during your working life, you may find yourself faced with a choice between taking a job you find personally rewarding but that does not pay well, or accepting a less satisfying job in a higher pay range. To accept the lesser paying job does not necessarily mean you have fallen into underearning. The question you would have to ask yourself is: *If I accept this job, can I make enough to meet my financial obligations or would this job undermine my financial strength and leave me with money problems? Does this job hinder my ability to take care of myself financially? Am I making conscious choices?*

When I was growing up, my mom decided to take a job working for our church headquarters, and did so knowing she would make less money than in the corporate world. When I told her I planned to write this book, she asked me, "Did you think I was underearning by working for the church?" The answer was no!

Remember, underearning is about making less then one needs. My mom made more than enough for a comfortable life, knew that our family's needs were being met, contributed to her retirement, and felt great satisfaction in her work. Understanding her economic situation—what I call "financial clarity"—allowed her the freedom to choose a job she found to be worthwhile and rewarding over one with more income that would have bought us a few extra luxuries but less satisfaction in her life.

What is most perplexing about underearning, more than how relative it is, is that it usually contains a paradox. Usually, underearners outwardly desire to make more money, but can't seem to turn this desire into reality. They confess to being clueless as to why they cannot turn their hard work and desire to succeed into earning more. Why is a genuine desire and seeming willingness to make more money usually not enough? The answer lies in examining all the unconscious motivations and beliefs that shape and direct one's actual behavior.

As you will see, the psychology behind underearning is complex. At the heart of underearning lie self-depriving behaviors that are often wrapped in the mantle of what I call "noble poverty." There are also complex, and often unacknowledged, reasons as to why underearning actually serves one's interests. And too, there is often a belief that if we only wait long enough, Prince Charming will come to our rescue. But because most people don't want to look at these potentially painful issues, they find ways not to. It is our unconscious beliefs and attitudes, which we will explore in Chapters 2, 3, and 4, that drive our underearning behavior. And because women do not want to see this behavior, and don't want to think about these beliefs, they lose themselves in vagueness and fog. In fact, as you will see in Chapter 5, being vague about money actually enables you to continue underearning.

Genuine self-evaluation is essential if you are to break this cycle of underselling yourself. Sure, it may be easier to blame conditions beyond your control for your lack of earning potential. Underearners may argue that the amount they earn is determined by economic factors out of their control, or gender discrimination, but this line of thinking fosters "victimhood." And it is easy to see how this sense of helplessness can lead to a host of other problems, such as depression, alcoholism, and other dysfunctions. However, when people honestly search for ways in which they might be responsible for their own underearning, they realize that they *can* do something about the problem. They can recapture that lost power and find themselves on the road to psychological and financial health.

Of course, taking responsibility brings its own challenges. Many women might see this as adding yet more work to their already unmanageable workload. A busy sales executive protests, "I can't possibly do any more!" Every hour of her hectic day is spoken for. But using this as an excuse is an outdated and ineffectual way of looking at the problem. Women have bought into the theory that they must work harder, update their skills, or change to a more promising career—in short, accomplish more if they ever expect to get ahead. But underearning cannot be solved by putting in longer hours or increasing one's portfolio of skills. Working harder is usually not the answer. If it were, this debilitating condition would not be so prevalent.

To overcome your pattern of underearning, you must first admit that something is not working, and then consider making a change—and that can be a scary proposition. The very idea of change can be overwhelming. You may feel threatened by trying a different approach, intimidated by the idea of assuming control of your destiny—these are both very real and reasonable reactions. Certainly it would be safer for you to just throw up your hands and say, "I'm doing the best I can!" But, while you may experience fear of failure at trying something new, the bigger risk is refusing to confront those issues you may have allowed yourself to ignore.

Other women have overcome their underearning, and you can too. Throughout this book, you will get to know many different women who struggle with underearning. We will follow them as they explore their patterns of underearning, and examine some of the reasons behind their behavior. Among the women you will meet are Mary, an administrative assistant who feels hopelessly locked into a low-paying job and paycheck-to-paycheck existence, and Teresa, a well-regarded therapist who knows she should be making more than she is, but continues to just get by. We'll meet Kristine, a young architect who suspects there are deeper reasons behind her inability to finish projects or market herself, and we'll meet Eleanor, who works for a nonprofit organization in which she believes passionately, and whose uneasy relationship with money keeps her forever on the edge of financial disaster.

These women, along with thousands more, are locked into a pattern of underearning. Sick of just getting by, they want to make more money—enough money to cover their needs and free them from continual financial worry. Yet, try as they might, they just can't. Some of them struggle with self-esteem issues that affect their earning potential. Others come to realize that repeatedly earning less than they need benefits them in some way. And almost all of them engage in behaviors that foster their underearning habit without their realizing that they are doing so.

Their stories will uncover ways of underearning you may never have considered and give insight into the many reasons why women fall into this trap, both consciously and unconsciously. But, most importantly, you will see how these women have overcome their underearning, and learn how you can do the same.

The First Step

The ways in which women underearn are as varied as the women themselves. Sometimes what they do to underearn is obvious; other times, their behavior that leads to underearning is almost impossible to detect, remaining hidden and unconscious until the underearner pursues discovery through honest self-evaluation.

I know this can be a tender topic, which, of course, only serves to keep it concealed. After all, who wants to admit to being an underearner? To do so leads to daunting questions: What's wrong with me? Why can't I earn more? Where did I go wrong? Just thinking that you've fallen into the underearning trap can bring on feelings of frustration and of being overwhelmed.

The good news is that when you acknowledge your underearning, you take the first step toward unlocking your earning potential. When you are conscious of your behavior and understand how it affects your entire life, you hold the key to solving the problem.

So let's look at some common ways women underearn and decide which ones you identify with. Once you've spotted your own underearning, you can look at the reasons that cause you to continue underselling yourself. This list is not meant to be exhaustive. It is merely a starting point to get you thinking about underearning in your own life. As you read the descriptions of these common forms of underearning, see what other examples come to mind.

Are You An Underearner?

As you read through the rest of this chapter, take a pencil and put a check next to the examples of underearning with which you identify. You may find that you've engaged in some of these behaviors consistently throughout your working life; others you may have done only occasionally or not at all. Remember, this is only for you. No one else will see it. So, take a deep breath and dive in.

❑ Avoiding Asking for a Raise

Of all the ways people underearn, this is probably the most common. In the ideal world, no one would have to ask for a raise. An employer would notice each employee's good work and reward her fairly and promptly, perhaps even with a smile and a thank you. However, in the real world, an employee must watch out for herself.

Mary, an office manager for a construction firm, wanted to make more money. Because her boss never brought up the subject, she knew she would have to be the one to do so, which meant asking him directly for a raise. As she considered this, Mary thought back to how she had handled the problem before, but she couldn't remember the last time she asked for a raise. The fact was, she never had. Whenever she had thought about approaching her boss about the subject, she would be overcome with anxiety and a fear of rejection. Rather than risk being turned down, she had never actually asked for what she wanted.

To rationalize her avoidance, Mary told herself that she would ask for that raise someday. She would simply wait for the right time—the perfect opportunity. Of course, that golden moment never seemed to come, and so she continued to do nothing.

❑ Neglecting to Raise Fees

For the self-employed, avoiding raising fees is the number one way to underearn. It is comparable to an employee not asking for a raise, although there can be more at stake. It's one thing to ask an employer for a raise; the biggest risk to the employee comes from simply being turned down, not losing her job. It is quite another thing, however, for the self-employed person to decide to give herself a raise. She must pass on that increase to her clients, and often times she fears she will create resentment and possibly even lose business. Many professionals find this risk almost impossible to take.

For some people, this behavior stems from not wanting to be involved with the financial side of their business. For example, an attorney in private practice certainly would prefer to focus on practicing law rather than dealing with fee structures and the company bottom line.

Raising fees presents a complex problem for many reasons and is particularly difficult for those in the "helping professions." Teresa, a therapist, complained that she was always living paycheck to paycheck, and she was sick of it. She had spent years in school, earning her certification as a professional therapist. She thought that once she began her practice, her years of hard work would pay off and money would cease to be a problem. But because she felt guilty asking for more money from the very people she was supposed to be helping, this was not the case.

❏ Giving Time Away

Our time is one of our most precious assets. Yet many people feel compelled to give it away to others, excessively in some cases, and at the expense of not using it to enrich their own lives and reach their goals.

Am I suggesting that it is always bad to give your time away? Of course not. But asking yourself *why* you do so might open your eyes. Are you consciously contributing your time for something you believe in? Or are you giving away your time because you undervalue yourself? Whenever you invest more time in a project than you are paid to, you need to check in with yourself to see if you are underearning.

Chances are that if you regularly put other people before yourself, you probably give away your time inappropriately or excessively. For women, who often are the caregivers in a family, the habit of putting others first is hard to break. It can feel uncomfortable to put your own needs and wishes first. But learning not to give your time away is essential. It ultimately comes down to the fact that valuing your time is the same thing as valuing yourself. The following two examples of underearning are examples of giving yourself and your time, away.

Excessive Volunteering

When I suggest to clients that their volunteering could be a form of underearning, I am often met with some very heated reactions. That's understandable; many of us feel strongly about our favorite causes, organizations, and issues, and we gladly contribute our time and money to support them.

Because this subject is fraught with emotion and misconception, let me be clear: I am not recommending that people give up volunteering, nor am I saying that all volunteering is a form of underearning. But when someone uses volunteering as a means of habitually giving away her knowledge, skills, and experience—in essence, undervaluing herself—then, yes, it becomes a problem.

If this scenario sounds familiar, then ask yourself: *Could these same skills I give away make me money if directed elsewhere? Is my volunteering time hurting my ability to earn what I need?*

Judy, for example is an experienced and efficient event planner, having worked with large and influential companies to design and organize events—anything from executive cocktail parties to industry-wide conferences. She did a great job and enjoyed a large clientele. Judy also put her talents to work as a volunteer for several different causes, such as orchestrating fundraising for the local domestic violence program and overseeing all of her church's events throughout the year.

With her busy life, Judy began to feel stressed out as she tried to fulfill all her commitments. As successful as she was, she often complained to friends that money was tight and she wished she made more. What Judy couldn't see was that the excess time and energy she had spent on volunteer projects could have been devoted to improving her financial situation.

Only you can decide how you spend your time; you may choose to work on projects that are worthy even though you know you won't be paid for your time and efforts. But here's a question you need to ask yourself: *Is your volunteering in any way affecting your ability to seek work that pays appropriate compensation?* If giving away your time means that you cannot make the amount of money you want, you may be underearning.

Underbilling

Another common form of underearning is underbilling, the practice of charging a client less than what is rightfully owed. I believe that underbilling is an epidemic among professionals. Whenever I discuss it in an underearning seminar, I can see the audience nodding their heads as they think about their own billing practices. Whether self-employed or working for a company, it can be difficult to charge clients the full amount owed.

Kristine, an architect with a small firm, was always busy and productive, and typically juggled several clients at a time. When faced with drawing up invoices, however, Kristine would alternate between feelings of guilt—she should have done more work in less time—and generosity—she could win points by giving the client a break. And she often gave away her time to people who dropped by or called her on the phone with "quick" questions, questions that often took an hour of her time. She knew she could have rightfully charged the client, but she couldn't bring herself to do it. With this attitude she invariably billed for fewer hours than she really put in on a project.

Kristine felt all this "good will" assured that the firm's clients would be happy with her and feel they were getting a good deal, and they were—at the expense of Kristine's financial stability. Not only was Kristine undervaluing her own services and making far less than the firm's other architects, but because the company took a percentage of her billable hours, she was not contributing to the financial success of the firm as a whole, which essentially put her job in jeopardy.

☐ Bartering

Bartering is another practice that illustrates just how insidious underearning can be.

At first glance, bartering seems to be both thrifty and resourceful, an efficient way to exchange goods and services on a simple, practical, straightforward level. But when people barter excessively, this behavior translates into a consistent lack of revenue—often hurting their business and their bottom line. Like volunteering, the basic concept of bartering is good; but to use it effectively takes diligence and discipline. Barterers often find that they have traded away their precious time and skills for something they may not need or want. And even those who receive services that they *can* use have to be careful that they aren't trading an inequitable amount of time or skill. So make sure you can use the service, and that you are trading time and money appropriately.

Throughout the years, I've noticed a trend among professionals who barter excessively: they tend to have an uneasy relationship with money. Consider Eleanor, who works for a nonprofit organization involved in a variety of good causes and who barters quite frequently. She had previously worked as a massage therapist, but gave it up because she wasn't making enough money, and she wanted to "make a difference" in the world. Now, whenever possible, she trades massages for whatever service she needs. She barters for the tune up on her car, for landscaping at her home, even for bread from the corner bakery.

Like a lot of people who barter, Eleanor found a source of pride in how frugal she was. Not only was she saving money, she was circumventing that "horrible money system." But she consistently bartered for items that were worth less than the cost of a typical massage—in essence, underselling herself. But because money did not enter directly into the picture, she was unable to see this. As we will see, Eleanor was underearning and falling into the trap of "noble poverty," where a part of you believes that there is virtue in not having money.

❏ Failure to Market Yourself

If it could be said that I have a "favorite" underearning trap, this would be it, as I have been on both sides: I teach people how not to fall into it, and have fallen into it myself.

Marketing oneself is essential for the self-employed as well as those on a salary, but still many business people find ways to avoid doing it. Not only do they dislike having to market themselves, they often don't know how. Judy, the special events planner, lamented, "I can't believe in all the time I was in school, no one ever taught me how to get started or find clients." I've heard the same complaint from lawyers, auto mechanics, chiropractors, massage therapists, and computer consultants, to name a few. No matter what a woman's profession may be, constantly working on how to sell herself can cause a lot of stress and discomfort. Most people simply want to do what they were trained to do, not spend time drumming up business. But, anyone who is self-employed simply can't make money without clients—and that takes marketing.

Although it's not as readily apparent, marketing is just as important for people in salaried jobs. They have to learn to be their own advocate if they expect to get ahead. Remember Mary, the administrative assistant? Like so many people, she simply did her job and waited to be noticed, then quietly resented it when she was passed over for promotions and raises. She felt she worked a lot harder than many of the people she watched move up the ranks, yet she was going nowhere. Employers respect people who stick up for themselves, are organized, and can point to their accomplishments. Employees who are too timid to "toot their own horn" are often seen as being indecisive or inconsequential in the high-rolling business world. Even worse, they may not be seen at all.

❏ Quitting a Job Prematurely

Quitting your job does not necessarily connote underearning. Sometimes, it is necessary to move on, for any of a variety of reasons. But if you quit prematurely, before you have gained everything you could from a position—skills and experience that could help you in your continued career development—you may be underearning. So it is almost never wise to quit a job without a new source of income. And as the old saying goes, it's always easier to get a job if you have a job.

Sometimes, people reach a point of feeling that their job is intolerable. When they can stand it no longer, they quit. Then, without a job, they start looking for a new one. If you are discontent in your job, it is far better to begin looking for better employment while you still employed. You will be job-hunting from a position of strength and will not feel as financially vulnerable. Otherwise, you may be temped to take the wrong job, because you find yourself in a position of having to bring in money, regardless of whether the job pays enough and is the right fit.

❏ Staying in a Position Too Long

While it is important to not quit a job prematurely without a game plan in place, many women have the opposite problem. Thousands of women stay in positions for far too long. Even though it becomes apparent that they will never get a decent raise, or get promoted, they stay in the hopes that things will get better. Sometimes it is because they have reached the top of their pay scale or job promotion possibilities, and the only way to advance is to move on to another company. Sometimes the job was a dead-end job in the first place, and it never had promotion possibilities. Other times, the job started out promising, but it became apparent at some point that it would not lead to better things. Perhaps you acquired a new boss who did not have your best interests in mind and was not supportive of your continued skill development and job advancement.

Sometimes, women like their work environment and feel intense loyalty to their employers, who consistently reward them with praise for their work and "thanks for a job well done," instead of giving their employee more money, the highest form of praise for a productive employee. Or women may be continually promised a raise, but it never actually happens, due to "budget cuts and freezes" and all sorts of other reasons. Women tend to be far too understanding of these situations, and will continue working and giving their best, long past the point when others would have moved on to a better company. Always, we hope it will get better, and we wait and wait, instead of taking action.

❑ Overlooking Marketable Skills

This form of underearning is particularly difficult to spot, for it's easy to sell oneself short and not even notice. While it may not cause outright job loss, it does make moving forward slow and difficult.

Eleanor, our barterer, wanted to work for a worthy cause. She had at one time been a fully qualified CPA, earning a good living. But at some point, she felt she wanted more meaning in her life and had grown tired of looking at numbers and tax returns. She wanted to connect with people at a deeper level, and so she decided to do something completely different and go to massage school. This next career was short lived, for she found it too physically taxing, and she had a difficult time earning enough money, even for her own modest needs. So she moved on to a nonprofit organization that did work she admired and in which she believed. She found herself performing whatever job needed to be done: office assistant, fundraiser, gofer, and general campaigner for the cause.

In her late 50s and making very little money, Eleanor often wished she had more income. Living from paycheck to paycheck was tiring and distressing, and it distracted her from the work she wanted to accomplish. Yet she already possessed the solution to her problem: She could make money using her accounting skills. In all the time she had worked for the nonprofit, she never tried to help them with their bookkeeping, though they needed this service desperately. While Eleanor worried about not having money as she tried to save the world, she never thought to use her expertise to do both.

If you have a skill that could potentially help you in your current job, have you thought of a way where you could incorporate it into your work or somehow use it to your benefit?

☐ Seeking Work for Which You Are Not Qualified

Applying for jobs for which an applicant is not qualified poses several problems: not only is it a waste of time and money, it can lead to missed opportunities for real and meaningful employment that may never be recouped.

Tina, a recently divorced artist with a divorce settlement in the bank, couldn't understand why her job search was so unsuccessful. Armed with her recent bachelor's degree in art history, she put in a lot of time and effort applying for jobs as an art director at local schools and museums. Even though most of the jobs she applied for preferred that applicants possess a master's degree in fine arts, Tina rationalized this away by telling herself she could do just as well as anyone with a graduate degree.

With no callbacks and no prospects, Tina felt frustrated. Yes, she worked hard at job hunting, but, as the song says, she was looking in all the wrong places. Her inability to assess her skills realistically and search for an appropriate job kept her from starting down the road to success.

☐ Turning a Blind Eye to Opportunity

This sounds broad, and, indeed, it is! Opportunity is all around us. What we choose to see is up to us. But opportunity often entails risk or making some sort of change, and change can be uncomfortable and stressful.

Teresa, the therapist, would periodically complain to her friends about not earning enough. During one such conversation a friend mentioned a job opportunity at a mental health center run by the local university. She thought it paid quite well, and urged Teresa to check it out. Although Teresa acted interested and promised to follow up, she never did. She assumed that the job would be either low paying or include work she didn't care to do. She wasn't even willing to make a short phone call to find out more information. Such an action could have led to an interview, perhaps a new job, and, ultimately, change. Teresa, evidently, did not want to change.

As we will discuss later in the book, people often underearn to serve themselves in some way. If underearning is somehow benefiting you, or if you don't think you are worthy of a better job, then chances are many opportunities to earn more have slipped through your fingers unnoticed.

❏ Not Preparing for the Future

We all know, at some level, that we must prepare ourselves financially for the future. But isn't that an investment/retirement issue, and not an underearning issue? The problem is that the devastating effects of underearning often don't truly catch up to us until the future, when we have less money on which we live. For many women, it is because they did not take advantage of retirement opportunities that were available to them when they were working.

When we think about how much money we are making at our jobs, we must take into account our entire compensation packages, not just our salaries or hourly rates. Retirement investing in the form of 401(k)s and 403(b)s are part of these packages. They should be considered part of your overall earnings. And many retirement plans have "matching" funds, meaning the company you work for will contribute, dollar for dollar, into an employee's retirement account, up to a certain percentage. That's free money!

LaDonna, a corporate accounts executive, lamented not taking advantage of this opportunity. She had held many jobs in the past several years, the kind of "serial employment" that has become more and more common. She had worked for four different companies in the past 10 years, each time for two or three years. At the first job, she needed to wait six months before she was eligible to participate in their 401(k) plan. After the six months passed, she never got around to starting her 401(k) investing. The following year, she was at a new company. Still, she did not get around to taking advantage of their retirement plan. Three years later, she continued her inaction at yet a third company. Now, in her 40s, she lamented all the money she had lost.

"It just makes me sick when I think about all the money I left on the table. I kept saying I'd get around to it, but I didn't know who to see, or what to do, and I was really busy. And it felt like every time I decided to figure it all out, I was at a new company again. Just think—that's 10 years when I could have been investing for my future. I kick myself every time I think about it."

Even if your job does not have retirement benefits, it is still important to make sure you are making enough money to be able to invest money in your own retirement. If you are earning enough to cover your needs, but not enough to save for your retirement, you may be underearning. We will explore this in Chapter 6, when we discuss just how much "enough" really is.

A Starting Point

If you recognized yourself in some of these scenarios, you might be feeling a bit overwhelmed or depressed as you realize all the ways in which you've underearned. While that's a natural reaction, I urge you to move past it and focus your attention on remedying the problem. The point of recognizing underearning is not to feel bad about it, but to learn how to break its cycle. To do that, you must become aware of *what* you are doing, as well as *why* you are doing it. You can begin that process with the following exercise.

✎ **Exercise: Cataloging Your Underearning** ✎
Using this chapter as a guideline, list every way you
can think of that you have underearned in your life.
You might ask a trusted friend for his or her observa-
tions, as others often see things that we can't. (A common reaction is, "Why didn't you tell me?") List specific
instances when possible.

Once you have your list, go back through it and
break down your experiences of underearning into two
categories: "Active Underearning" and "Passive Underearning." (Remember, active underearning is defined
as doing something specific to continue underearning,
such as giving your time away; passive underearning
refers to a lack of action that leads you to continue
underearning, such as not asking for a raise.) Keep this
list with you as you go through this book. You will probably add more to it as you continue to read.

Admitting you are underearning is the first step in your
journey. Recognizing your behavior is of paramount importance in overcoming it. Once you are willing to admit you may
be underearning, you are ready for the next step, and that is to
begin to understand why you do what you do. In the next few
chapters, you will be analyzing your belief systems and assumptions that have led you to underearn in the first place. It is time
to turn inward and begin to assess the unconscious beliefs that
may be fueling your behavior.

Chapter Two

The Illusion of Noble Poverty

"I'm sick of always living paycheck to paycheck, but I just don't see how it's possible for me to ever make enough money."

Eleanor sat slumped in my office, telling me of her history with money and why she finally decided to enter into financial counseling.

"It's not like I have a lot of debt, but it's always there. In fact, I don't remember ever *not* having debt. But that wouldn't even be an issue if I made enough money. I guess at my age it's too late. And besides, I believe in the work I do."

Most people might be surprised to hear Eleanor's lament. An attractive and energetic woman in her late 50s, she certainly seemed to live a full life. Divorced many years ago, she had carved a career for herself in the nonprofit sector, in which she not only worked full-time but also volunteered for numerous charities and programs in the city. Her personal life included getting together with her three grown children, attending on-going classes on personal growth and hiking. All who knew her admired her competence, energy, and ability to juggle several different projects at once. Yet she saw herself as a woman who constantly struggled financially, who never had enough.

"I'm just tired of being anxious about money all the time. I don't know if it's possible for me to make more, but I want to break out of this pattern of pretending not to be worried about the future when, in fact, I'm *very* worried."

We all know someone like Eleanor—someone who says she would like to have more money, yet always opts for the low-paying service jobs. Or perhaps they devote their time and efforts to their favorite cause for little or no money. Maybe they just seem to repel money when it does come into their life, possibly by giving it away, while still being frustrated with living from paycheck to paycheck. This impoverished condition can be a form of underearning I call "noble poverty."

Of all the many faces of underearning, noble poverty is one of the most insidious, for it is often camouflaged by other issues and unconscious beliefs. For example, many women feel that money is somehow tainted, that having money can actually be seen as negative. Of course, this belief is usually unconscious. Like most underearners, those wrapped up in noble poverty frequently espouse their desire for more money, complaining about not having enough and venting their frustration at always struggling to make ends meet. But overriding those surface concerns is the deep-seated and unconscious belief that truly drives the person's behavior: to have money is somehow wrong. In fact, it can be corrupt and immoral. Hence, I would define noble poverty as "the continual practice of earning less than one needs based on the belief that there is virtue in not having money."

On the face of it, this kind of thinking seems preposterous. When first confronted with the idea of noble poverty, many of my clients are indignant. They respond with comments like "What do you mean I believe having money is bad? You must be kidding!"

But think about it. Many people believe there is spiritual, societal, or political virtue in keeping oneself poor. And there are aspects of noble poverty that seem to make sense, especially in this day and age of massive consumption and materialistic fervor. Many people—and I count myself among them—feel that as a nation we have gone the way of conspicuous consumption, which has led to our using a disproportionate amount of the world's resources. Many responsible people firmly believe that as a society, we *should* cut back, conserve resources, enjoy simpler and more balanced lives, and coexist in greater harmony with nature. But this philosophy does not equate with money being inherently bad.

You probably know people who live in noble poverty, who wear their frugality and self-denial as a badge of honor. They brag about how little money they spend, the so very few resources they use, the many ingenious ways they have found to save a buck here and there. Their lifestyle fairly shouts, "Look at me! See how little I can get by with!" They may not come right out and say it, but, yes, they see their financial situation as virtuous.

These same people may contend that they spend very little because they don't make enough money. But I would turn this statement around. Why do they not make enough money, so that they are forced to spend so little? Is it possible they created their lives in such a way as to prohibit themselves from having money? And are their actions the result of the beliefs they hold?

Nonprofit work provides some great examples of people who follow noble ideals without adequate financial compensation. Yes, I can hear the objections already—but don't get upset yet. Let me explain what I mean. Non-profit work is not the culprit. I support non-profit activities and organizations and, in fact, I worked for a wonderful non-profit for several years. But many women suffer from what I call "non-profititis." That is, they continually compromise their financial security in order to support the causes they believe in. They will take jobs in the non-profit sector without regard as to whether the monetary compensation is adequate for their needs. They believe that the cause—not the salary—is all that matters. Unfortunately, they soon find themselves in a precarious financial position.

Eleanor, for example, said that when she was younger, she never thought about the money. In fact, she said she had believed firmly that it should not be about the money, that if a job was about getting paid well, you must not be doing something worthwhile. The very idea that non-profits were set up to "not be profitable," made her more comfortable. "Once an organization is in it for the money, then you just can't trust them. At least, that's what I used to believe. I'm not so sure anymore...."

I do not believe that working for a non-profit will automatically threaten one's financial stability. But those who choose to work for a non-profit—or any organization—for less than they are worth, must reconsider their choice if they want to avoid underearning.

The most important point for you to consider is whether you can take care of yourself financially no matter where you find a position, be it in the non-profit sector or corporate world. Ask yourself this question: "Does taking this position undermine my ability to build financial security for myself?" With this kind of self-evaluation, you become conscious of the work you do *and* the money you earn. Only then can you become financially secure.

Belief Systems

It is fascinating to look at the complex beliefs of underearners, but before going into them, it is important to note that for many underearners, it has honestly never occurred to them that they could make more money. They may fret about their debt or the many expenses in their lives, and they may dislike their current jobs. But for many women, it honestly does not occur to them that one valid financial option for them is to increase the amount of money they are earning. I've heard many women say, as they've listened to me talk about underearning, that for them, it just honestly never occurred to them that they could make more. Opening up to this possibility is the first step. Wanting to make more, and then believing you can, is the place to start in overcoming underearning. Then it is helpful to look deep into your own underlying beliefs about earning money.

While the internal beliefs of underearners wrapped up in noble poverty can be complicated and laced with contradictory messages, the basic foundation remains constant—underearners have a love/hate relationship with money. They may like the things money can buy or enjoy the freedom money would give them, but because they find something inherently wrong with having money, they shy away from acquiring it.

Underearners who live a life of noble poverty often follow the maxim: "It is better to be good and poor, than rich and evil." In fact, many underearners dislike and mistrust those who have acquired wealth. They often assume that anyone who has made a lot of money must be unscrupulous, or the way in which the wealthy made their money must be unethical, or rich people in general cannot be "nice" people.

Sound a bit farfetched? Well, it's not. Take a moment to consider this: While you may think you don't have anything against the wealthy, have you ever said something derogatory about someone who is very well off? Bill Gates? Ted Turner? Oprah? In Barbara Stanny's book *Secrets of Six-Figure Women* (HarperCollins, 2002), she writes about an AARP survey of money attitudes that was done of 2,300 people over the age of eighteen—a full 40 percent of the women felt people who have a lot of money "are greedy, insensitive, and feel superior." Underearners make negative assumptions about those with money because a part of them finds having money to be objectionable. Therefore they can stop themselves from making good money because they rationalize it as a negative thing.

For many underearners, these feelings go back to childhood. Unfortunately, many people grow up in a home where money is a source of conflict. Some heard their parents fight constantly about money, and others lived with low levels of chronic financial stress. One client told me, "Everyone just knew to never go near dad when he was paying the bills." While children may not understand money and the complexities involved in household finance, they inevitably decide that whatever this money thing is, it must be bad. They equate money with conflict, unhappiness and sometimes violence. As adults, these people often want nothing to do with money. This is not a conscious thing. But unconsciously, matters of money make them feel stressed and uncomfortable.

I talked with San Francisco-based financial counselor, Kathryn Amenta, about this. She told me that many of her underearning clients say their families were full of conflict and high drama over money. "Many of them came from families where there was a lot of chaos in general, and often times I find that they will shut down over financial matters, if they become too overwhelmed by their feelings around money." Because of their discomfort around money, these underearners often want nothing to do with finance as an adult, and this has a direct impact on their ability to make good money. When people grow up so uncomfortable with money, they become suspicious of people who do have money.

In a session with Teresa, an experienced therapist, I brought up the concept of underearning. We discussed the possibility of raising her rates, to which she was quite resistant. When I asked her what other therapists in the area charged, her reply was scornful.

"Oh, I know some real big-shot therapists who charge $105 an hour, but I think there is something unscrupulous about them. I don't know anything for sure, but I'll just bet there's something going on there. I wouldn't feel right charging that much money."

Although Teresa didn't actually know of anything dishonest, as she herself admitted, she was making the assumption that a therapist who makes good money is somehow doing something wrong. This type of thinking is especially prevalent among those who have chosen a career in the "helping" professions, such as teachers, nurses, therapists, etc. Women in these occupations often have a difficult time charging adequately for their services. The people who come to them need help; charging those people for providing that help can seem cold and hard-hearted.

So what are some of the many messages underearners live with? Many of them are clichés we all know, drummed into our heads long ago by hard-working parents, so familiar that we no longer hear them or think about them. When I ask people at my seminars to brainstorm different messages they heard growing up, the same ones always surface: "Money doesn't grow on trees." "What do you think I am, made of money?" And my personal favorite, "There just isn't enough."

Some money sayings are religiously inspired, such as "Money is the root of all evil." (However, as many people know, this is a misquote; the Bible actually says "The *love* of money is the root of all evil.") And, of course, there's the well-worn parable that pronounces "It is easier for a camel to pass through the eye of a needle than for a rich man to enter heaven." It is as if our common religious beliefs tell us that money is sinful, and we are encouraged to wait for the afterlife to experience perfect abundance.

✎   **Exercise: Money Messages**   ✐

Think for a moment about the house in which you grew up. What were the messages you heard about money? You may not even know exactly where some of those messages came from, but you know you heard them. What did the people around you say about money, and what did they think of the wealthy? What did you learn from your parents about money that was never said aloud? In your journal, begin to compile a list of money sayings and beliefs. You may remember offhand remarks or rules of the house, such as "We do not discuss money." Try to write down two or three in your journal. As you think of more, come back to this list and continue compiling it.

Remember Eleanor from the beginning of the chapter? She could not think of any money messages she inherited, except for the overall impression that there was never enough. Yet when I asked her about her childhood, there was a lot to tell that related to money issues. She grew up in North Dakota, the oldest of five children. Her father was a laborer in the oil fields and didn't make much, so money was always tight. Eleanor's clearest memories of childhood are of her parents fighting about money. Her mother would accuse her father of squandering money on himself, and she would have to beg for money to run the household, which she hated doing.

As a result, Eleanor's mother became extremely frugal, finding countless ways to save money. She sewed as many of the kids' clothes as she could; what couldn't be made at home was bought at the cheapest of shops, including the one new pair of shoes the children got each year. She recalls her mother poring over the newspaper looking for sales and second-hand items, for bargains and coupons to clip. Eleanor vividly remembers the time her mother sent her to the store to buy bread. When she returned with her carefully bought purchase, her mother berated her for spending too much and not going to a cheaper store.

Let's look at some of the possible messages Eleanor the child received about money:

ॐ Money creates conflict between people.

ॐ There is never enough money.

ॐ It is a virtue to get by with as little as possible.

ॐ Money is, somehow, inherently bad.

It's not unusual for kids who grow up seeing their parents fight about money to want nothing to do with money as an adult. Even if they didn't fully understand the issues as a child, as an adult they still associate money with having caused their parents' conflicts and, ultimately, an unpleasant home environment. In Eleanor's case, however, I believe the strongest message she came away with, the one that most impacted her adult life, was that to have just enough to "get by" was a virtue. Following this message led, in part, to her consistent underearning.

We all have many messages about earning and money concealed within the fabric of our childhoods. As you continue the previous exercise on money messages (page 49), try to remember different events, asking yourself: *What message would this incident give a little girl about money and earning? How has this affected me as an adult?*

Artists especially fall prey to noble poverty—they see their impoverished condition as a sign that they are "true artists." And artists that do well financially are often portrayed as having sold out. Tina saw herself as an artist and had a very conflicted relationship with money. She was frustrated with having to make money in the first place. (It is as if artists have been given a special dispensation exempting them from having to make enough money.) But her perception of herself reflects our culture: Somehow artists aren't expected to make a lot of money. In fact, this lack of monetary success is often an integral part of their self-image. "Starving" and "artist" naturally go hand in hand.

Like other underearners engaged in noble poverty, Tina saw two worlds, the internal world—that is, the world of spirit and art—and the external world of greed and crass consumerism. When she was younger, she loudly espoused her beliefs about mainstream society as being superficial and overly materialistic. She was so strong in her convictions that she actively disliked anyone she felt lived only in this "soulless" outer world. She lived her life in the other extreme, identifying only with the inner world. Art, not money, was all that mattered. Later, when she ended up marrying a business major, she tempered somewhat. After all, her husband lived in this external world of "greed and consumerism." But ironically, this allowed Tina to continue believing in the impoverished artistic way, because her new husband was supporting them. As an "artist," she felt no pressure to make money, because her husband paid most of the bills.

Unfortunately, when people split the "internal" world from the "external" world, an uneasy relationship to money invariably follows. They categorize financial matters as belonging to the external world and equate having money to being materialistic. And even though these people are forced to live in the external world, they can show their disdain for it by staying as far away from money (and what it represents to them) as possible.

Like many artists, Tina's greatest fear was that of not being true to herself. Her opposition to the acquisitive society in which she lived, and the role money played within it, made it impossible for her to acquire and keep money herself, because to do so would have compromised her beliefs. Unfortunately, as you will see, her marriage did not last, and she was forced, once again, to look at the money question.

✎   Exercise: Journal Questions   ✎
In your journal, answer the following questions:

1. Do I think/feel there is some virtue in being poor?

2. "It's better to be good and poor, than rich and evil?" Do I find any truth to the statement? Are these the only options?

3. How do I really feel about the wealthy?

To look more deeply into the lives of underearners engaged in noble poverty is to often find a world filled with physical deprivation. Many underearners live in homes with old furniture, wear worn-out clothes, and drive jalopies. In essence, they put off buying things that many of us would consider essential or commonplace.

Eleanor, for example, rented a small, one-bedroom apartment in a dilapidated building. Even though she often felt nervous walking at night through the run-down neighborhood in which she lived, she would never have dreamed of giving up her place because the rent was so cheap. To pay more money when she didn't really have to just seemed wrong to her. The inside of her apartment reflected this same thinking, furnished as it was with finds from thrift shops and the cast-offs of friends who had bought newer furniture.

"It's okay," she assured me. "I like it just fine. After all, it's just me."

Her actions, however, belied her true feelings, for she confessed that she hesitated to entertain all but her closest friends at her place, in part because she felt self-conscious about how the place looked. She mentioned that her one wish was to buy herself a new mattress, as the old one she slept on now hurt her back. Still, she just couldn't bring herself to put out "that kind of money."

Yet Eleanor espoused her way of life as a path she had chosen. She said she wanted to live a simple life, to engage in "voluntary simplicity." But as you will see, this is more complicated then it seems at first glance.

Voluntary Simplicity

I have found that sometimes, people confuse voluntary simplicity with noble poverty, so let's talk for a moment about the concept of "voluntary simplicity." To engage in voluntary simplicity means to consciously choose a simpler lifestyle that requires less money.

Voluntary simplicity, a term coined by Duane Elgin, author of the book by the same name, has developed into a popular movement. Its philosophy of simplifying and downscaling one's life has been taken up and espoused by thousands of people.

Many of whom are tired of being part of the stressful, complicated, overly materialistic culture in which we live and their goal is to get back to basics.

Many advantages come with engaging in voluntary simplicity, not the least of which is more freedom. How can that be? Because living with fewer "must haves" means reducing the need to generate money to support those desires.

Some people have lived within the philosophy of voluntary simplicity for decades. Others, burned out and disillusioned with corporate American life and its excessive and expensive lifestyle, have just discovered this lifestyle. Its attraction is understandable: Those who slow down, reduce stress, desire less, and live more simply may, in the long run, live a freer and more contented life.

You may be wondering what voluntary simplicity has to do with trying to make more money, or its connection to noble poverty. If you take another look at its definition, you will find the words "consciously choose." This is what lies at the heart of voluntary simplicity—a willful preference for a particular way of life. And although it is a valid and real choice for many, for others it is camouflage. In my experience, there are underearners who say they are voluntarily—meaning *consciously*—living a simpler life, when in fact they have been *unconscious* about their earnings—and their relationship to money—for a long time.

This lack of awareness creates a poorer lifestyle, and when one "wakes up" to the reality of the situation, it can be very painful. A sudden and frank realization—of the shabby belongings, the worn clothes, the lack of funds for activities or even necessities—can be devastating.

Some underearners who find themselves in these circumstances rationalize their situation away. "I'm not really poor," they tell themselves. "I have chosen this life. I am choosing to live more simply." But, sadly, this is often not the truth.

To determine which is true for you—whether your lifestyle is voluntary or involuntary—ask yourself this: Have you consciously chosen the way you live, or did you wake up to your lifestyle and then put a more appealing label on it? Admittedly, this is a difficult question, one that may take some time and genuine soul-searching to answer honestly.

A variation on the misrepresented concept of voluntary simplicity is the romanticization of poverty. Many women are prone to fantasies about the simple joy of living on little income. They envision their older selves, puttering away contently in their charming gardens, volunteering their time to worthy causes, wanting little and needing less, but always living comfortably. Unfortunately, the reality is much bleaker, given statistics on women's retirement funding. Although women will actually need more in retirement than men (because they live, on average, seven years longer than men), few are adequately prepared. According to the National Center for Women and Retirement Research, over 58 percent of female baby boomers have less than $10,000 saved in some form of retirement savings. This is particularly alarming because it is estimated that 80 percent to 90 percent of women will be solely responsible for their finances, at some point in their lives. (Nintey percent of women end up single, divorced, or widowed.)

Many women find comfort in a rationalization, rather than realization, of what their future will be. Instead of confronting their situations head on, they stick their heads in the sand and hope all will be well. But, in fact, all may not be well—they need to wake up and truly understand just what path they're headed down. That may be a harsh assessment, but it is a far better course than sitting back and doing nothing, which is what so many women choose to do.

Of course, nothing is black and white; every situation is complicated by an array of factors. In truth, there can be a fine line between anti-materialism and self-deprivation. The key is to be *conscious* of what you choose.

I believe that my mother-in-law, Grace, went about all of this in the right way. She is deeply spiritual, meditates regularly, and is one of the most conscious people I know. She belongs to a wonderful community of friends and has become active in the causes that appeal to her, and she has enough money to do what she wants. It may not be a lot of money by other people's standards, but coupled with her simple lifestyle, her retirement income allowed her to retire 10 years earlier than her peers.

Grace worked for the department of education in her state. She could have gone on to higher paying jobs in the corporate world, but she loved being involved in education—especially the decision-making—and had started many successful programs. She was smart, worked hard, followed her ideals, and—this is the important part—always made sure she was paid appropriately.

How did she do it? First of all, Grace knew what her position should pay, and she was not afraid to see that she was paid fairly. Second, she had a career plan. She always knew where she was trying to go and continued to invest in herself with education and training. Third, she managed her money wisely, taking advantage of the investment programs available to her. She always invested in her retirement and monitored it carefully. That was it. She didn't do anything fancy, didn't play the stock market, didn't inherit money. Slow and steady, she went along enjoying her life, her family, and her career, and focusing on her own interests.

One advantage Grace did have was in being introduced to and reading the seminal work *Your Money or Your Life*, by Vicki Robbins and Joe Dominguez, which discussed simplifying your life so you don't need as much money in the first place. Taking their advice to heart, she consciously simplified her life while she was still employed and investing. This sound strategy allowed her to retire at age 55. Of course, for Grace, "retired" means spending time pursuing her many interests, which include teaching meditation in the prison system, going on regular hikes with friends, and spending lots of time with her grandson. If Grace had not been as conscious about her earning, acquiring, and investing money, she would still be working—not devoting time to her favorite causes and enjoying the high quality of life that she does.

One day when my mother-in-law and I were discussing the concepts of voluntary simplicity and noble poverty, I asked whether she thought some people rationalized their impoverished lives by falsely claiming to live simply by choice. This was her reply:

> "Voluntary simplicity gives a deep sense of purpose and satisfaction. I think people locked in noble poverty—instead of practicing voluntary simplicity—feel highly stressed, dissatisfied, and find that they don't have the freedom to do what they want. In voluntary simplicity, there is a lack of stress, and a lot of freedom and joy. I get to choose how to spend my money. I may not have the newest car, but hey, I celebrated my 60th birthday by hiking in the Himalayas!"

✎ **Exercise: Journal Question** ✐

In your journal, think about the following question:
- Am I consciously choosing my life? Or, through indecision and passivity about money, has my life chosen me?

Self Deprivation

At its heart, engaging in noble poverty is a form of self-depriving behavior. "Self-depriving behavior" can be described as engaging in acts or pursuing activities, often subconsciously, that keep a person from enjoying something she values, such as time, money, achievement, love, etc.

Psychologist Susan Forward, author of the wonderful 1994 book *Money Demons* (Bantom, 1994), writes about this pattern of financial self-deprivation in which women are unable to spend money on themselves—even if they can afford to—without suffering tremendous feelings of guilt and anxiety. Forward describes these women as having their "receiving valve" stuck. This receiving valve is an unconscious control within each of us that dictates how comfortable we feel giving to ourselves and letting others give to us. But in a woman who feels undeserving, this receiving valve shuts down; she can give but not receive, because she sees herself as undeserving. And she will place herself in a financial position that guarantees she has little or no money to give to herself, using underearning to deprive herself of the comforts and joys of life that could be reasonably expected from a person earning at her potential.

Underearners fall into the habit of routinely shutting down their needs, and thus shrinking their lives. Let me give you an example:

> An underearner and an overspender both see a beautiful purse they would like to have but, for whatever reason, they cannot afford to buy. The overspender reacts by buying the purse anyway, perhaps by using a credit card, because she cannot stand the pain of being unable to have something. She may say to herself, "What's wrong with me that I can't afford that?" and then buys it to prove to herself that, yes, she really is deserving.The underearner on the other hand, responds to the urge to buy with a different point of view. She says to herself, "I don't really want that purse anyway," and walks away. She may go so far to scorn the item, and then feel superior. She is above that petty materialism. But this is classic underearner thinking, shutting down her desires and needs, convincing herself she doesn't really want or need whatever the item is. To admit she doesn't have enough money to buy

something most people could reasonably expect to afford is painful and even shameful, so denial is more comfortable—sort of a sour grapes syndrome grown large.

Both ways of dealing with the purchase of the purse are unhealthy. (As we all know, overspenders can wrack up enormous debt.) Because underearners do not have enough money, they respond to the gap in their life—between what they need or want and what they can actually afford—by denying that they want what they can't have. They shut down their desires to protect themselves from rejection and disappointment. Ron Gallen writes about this behavior in his 2002 book, *The Money Trap* (HarperCollins). He says that although an underearner may profess wanting money on the outside, unconsciously, they desire to keep the world as small and safe as possible in order to avoid disappointment. "Staying small so the world won't lop your head off—reject you—is the tried and true underlying theme of the underearner."

This "shrinking" of one's needs and wants because of a lack of money can lead to bigger problems. Once an underearner starts shutting down in one area of her life, she is more likely to deny her desires in other areas as well. And it's easy to see why. Underearners believe they do not deserve the object of their desires, which fuels their self-depriving behavior.

✎   **Exercise: Journal Questions**   ✐

In your journal, contemplate the answers to the following two questions. Try to be as honest as you can.

➡ Do I deprive myself of things I can really afford?

➡ Do I lead a restricted life due to a lack of money?

If you answered yes to these, chances are you are experiencing a lot of deprivation in your life. Don't despair. It is possible to overcome deprivation, through making better money, and through improving how you care for yourself. Chapter 7 will address self care and give you a practical way to address your deprivation through the creation of a "deprivation inventory."

Looking at Self-Esteem

The feeling of "undeservedness," which so many under-earners experience, is rooted in an underearner's sense of low self-esteem. I've worked with many women who I felt were extremely intelligent, capable, and competent in their chosen professions, who nonetheless suffered from the nagging feeling that maybe they weren't so good after all. Sometimes they express it as the Imposter Syndrome: "If they only knew how bad I really am, that I don't know everything, that I mess up all the time..." And because they never fully believe in themselves, they never believe they "deserve" to make top dollar. As this book will reveal, these women may even unconsciously sabotage themselves to make sure they don't make a lot of money. Occasionally, these underearners find themselves in a position where they are making good money, and it can haunt them. They can't shake the feeling that they don't really deserve all this money, and it is only a matter of time before someone finds out that they aren't all they are cracked up to be, and it is all taken away.

Where does low self-esteem come from? While the topic of self-esteem is too large to fully explore in a book such as this, let's discuss it briefly. In her book, *Breaking the Chain of Low Self-Esteem* (WolfPublishing, 1998), Marilyn Sorensen wrote that women with low self-esteem have a negative view of themselves based primarily on negative interpretations of past experiences, usually beginning in childhood and within the home environment. These women have believed the worst about themselves so strongly and for so long that they discard any positive feedback that contradicts this belief. So, for example, if the boss tells an employee with low self-esteem what a wonderful job she is doing, the employee doesn't believe him, thinking the boss either is simply being nice to her or has some ulterior motive. Such an employee can receive the most glowing evaluation and then privately discount the entire review, as it contradicts her negative view of herself. And, of course, because she honestly doesn't believe herself to be worthy or competent, this employee would never seek or expect a raise, which keeps her a perpetual underearner.

A woman with a healthy sense of self-esteem knows she deserves to earn an appropriate wage for the work she does. She can objectively view her work and gauge its worth, and then feel confident in asking for the right amount of compensation. Because she respects herself, she expects the same from others and is less likely to be trapped by those debilitating feelings that lead to underearning.

Difficult Questions

As you've seen, noble poverty can be insidious, camouflaged by complex issues and formed by unconscious beliefs from the messages received while growing up. Often hidden within childhood memories, these messages may be that money is somehow inherently bad or evil, or that it is virtuous to get by with as little as possible, and they can dramatically affect a person's ability to earn money. Only by examining these memories and pulling out these messages can someone stuck in noble poverty begin to see how her beliefs have shaped her financial behavior.

It's imperative to become aware of what you really think about money. These deeply-held beliefs influence our ability to earn enough money. This influence is farther reaching than most people realize, because underneath these unconscious beliefs is often poor self-esteem, and it is this low self-esteem that really keeps us from making good money, because we don't believe we *deserve* it.

In order to overcome underearning, we must begin to believe we deserve to make good money. So open yourself up to the possibility that money is a good thing, and you deserve plenty of it.

Chapter Three

From Prince Charming to the Bag Lady

For 20 years, Judy played the good wife. Married when she was 22, she raised three children and created a home environment where all could flourish. At the same time, she diligently helped her husband build the "family" business by assisting with reports, editing his work, and doing the accounting. This, in addition to 20 years of PTA meetings, dinner on the table by 6 p.m. and a home any woman would be proud of. Twenty years—and then it all fell apart.

When the dust settled and the divorce was finalized, she found herself in her mid-40s with teenage children, the home where they had lived, some child support, and a small amount of alimony until she could get "back on her own feet." She knew she needed to work, but for the last two decades her work had consisted of raising children and helping her husband in his business—a business she had believed belonged to both of them. Though he paid her a portion of the business assets in the divorce settlement, she knew he would continue growing the business for years to come.

Judy picked up the pieces—because she had to. She played on her ability to organize anyone and anything, and reinvented herself as a special events planner. Reinvention was what it was all about. And she was good at what she did.

But now, at age 60, Judy was forced to live on a restricted budget, and was angry that life had turned out this way. This was not the way it was "supposed" to be. Fifteen years had passed since her divorce, and she was beginning to realize she might never retire. Worse than that nebulous notion, however, were the nightmares which haunted her, in which she wandered the streets with a shopping cart full of her life's possessions and no one to care for her—a bag lady.

The Romance Myth

The Romance Myth is the myth that a woman will always be taken care of. It is a myth so basic, and so well ingrained, that many women do not recognize it for what it is—an outdated fairytale. It is the belief that if a woman does what she is supposed to do—that is, follow the rules that were set down for her—all will be well. At its most basic, the Romance Myth is based on the classical marital bargain. If a woman creates a home, raises children, and behaves properly, she will be provided for.

The Romance Myth plays on a woman's fear of being abandoned, and her secret wish to be rescued. It is predicated on the "doing the right thing" mentality, and that "right thing" means putting other people before herself. It is about taking care of others, at all costs. Collette Dowling writes, in her masterful book *Maxing Out* (Little, Brown and Company, 1998), that the Romance Myth is in essence about "protection in exchange for compliance with traditional female roles." It is the myth that if a woman only behaves "properly" by putting other people's needs before her own and giving up her own dreams and goals, she will be protected. She will not have to go out into the cruel world and fend for herself.

When Judy had been married for 10 years, she had debated going back to school. With her children at ages seven and nine, she was beginning to think of her future, and a dissatisfaction was growing in her life. What was she doing, and where was she going? She felt lost, and was beginning to feel trapped in her marriage. Maybe in school she could discover some new skills, and a new direction. But her husband had persuaded her to wait. "It isn't the right time. We don't have the money just now. What about the children? They need you." So Judy decided to do the "right thing," and wait. There would be time for school later...But as you will see, choosing to passively wait and see what the future may hold can be a terrible mistake.

One of the saddest results of the Romance Myth is that many women do not focus on actively planning their futures. Instead, they just wait and wait, hopeful that something will come about to ensure their happiness, and fearful that nothing will happen. So it is no surprise that, according to the National Center for Women and Retirement Research, nearly 70 percent of women say they have no idea how much they will need for retirement. Women are not taking charge of their futures, and I believe that holding on to the Romance Myth perpetuates this.

It has not always been like this for us. As little girls, we are full of dreams, desires, and plans for our futures. Ask any 8-year-old girl what she wants to be when she grows up, and she can give you an answer. "I want to be a ballerina." "I want to be a teacher." "I want to be a marine biologist." "I want to be a doctor." But something happens to these wonderfully alive and precocious girls when they enter adolescence. As they begin to develop physically, and their attention slowly turns to their futures as adults, the Romance Myth begins to take effect. Their confidence takes a battering in the classrooms and they become hesitant, in contrast to the boys who vie for the teacher's attention, shouting out their answers. Add to this the notion that so much of the attention given teenage girls is related to their sexuality and attractiveness, and slowly the door of the future swings closed, replaced with daydreams of wedding dresses and Mr. Right. Much has been written about this sad transformation. (Perhaps the best treatment of the subject is Peggy Orenstein's book *Schoolgirls: Young Women, Self-Esteem, and the Confidence Gap* [Anchor Books, 1994].)

For women who never marry, the Romance Myth can be a double-edged sword. Believe it or not, never marrying can actually be a good thing for a woman's financial health, given the rate of divorce, and other factors. But some unmarried women live as if they are in a permanent holding pattern. A part of them assumes, almost unconsciously, that of course they will not be alone their whole lives—that is not how they were told it would be. So they wait. This "waiting" wreaks havoc on their ability to care for themselves financially. They never fully pay attention to money, their earning power, and their net worth, because they persist in their belief that their finances will not always be all up to them.

Julie, who worked in a women's shelter, offered these comments: "I guess that in the back of my mind, I was thinking that someday I'd get married, have kids, and stay home with them while my husband worked. So the urgency to make money, to get ahead, just wasn't there. I think a part of me thought, why bother? It's not like I'll have to solely support myself my whole life. There will be someone else there too, someday."

When I first decided to write this book, I did not intend to include a chapter on the Romance Myth. Underearning, as I've said, centers on self-sabotage and what women do to themselves. Yet the Romance Myth is not entirely of women's own making, and I was loath to tackle this ephemeral myth that kept floating in the background of so many women's lives. But there it was. I see it at work in the lives of women of my mother's generation, as well as in the lives of my own friends. I am continually frustrated that we have not come farther, that so many women my own age still do not lay out a course for their own lives, but instead let life carry them along while they care for husbands and children, focused on making the lives of their loved ones better.

The Romance Myth undermines a woman's ability to take control of her financial destiny. It is nearly impossible for a woman to earn at her potential when a part of her is secretly waiting to be rescued. If she has an unconscious belief that it is not all up to her, that someday Price Charming will come riding into her life and take care of her (or she is already married to Prince Charming), she will not take her career seriously. She will not engage fully in career planning, and she certainly won't make sure that she is negotiating for top dollar. Why should she?

Many, many women were raised on the Romance Myth, and at times they feel the hapless victims of a fairytale gone bad. And to make matters worse, they're not really supposed to talk about it. In this day and age, women want to see themselves as being strong. A woman craves independence, freedom, and the ability to create any life she chooses. And if she craves independence, she can't admit that she is waiting for rescue. And so the myth continues to hover in the background, unexpressed and unacknowledged, free to wreak havoc with her financial life.

For years after the divorce, Judy found ways to make ends meet with her event planning business, because she had to. But when retirement issues loomed, she was faced with wondering why she had never taken her business to the next level. She had worked hard when she needed to, and provided the best she could for her children, but somehow, she had neglected to put anything away for the future.

"I guess I figured it was just impossible." But as she looked at her underearning issues, she began to see years of under pricing herself, coupled with never really focusing on marketing her business. She had always been so busy. Who had time to market? But of course, she had time for volunteer activities, social activities, and other time-consuming aspects of daily life.

"I guess I never really took my company that seriously. I just couldn't believe it was all up to me. I still can't. And it's just not fair! My ex-husband is already retired, and it makes me see red when I think about it. Why did things turn out like this?"

When it comes to the Romance Myth, I hear that question a lot. "Why did things turn out like this?" Women often complain, "This is not how it was supposed to be." But of course, things don't always turn out according to the Romance Myth.

My mother was a "full time" homemaker, as we would call her now. When I was 7 years old, she created a wonderful bedroom for me. She sewed matching curtains to go with my Raggedy Anne bedspread, and put up painted shelves for all my dolls and playthings. My little sister had her own wonderful bedroom down the hall. I loved spending time with my mom, and I was lucky she had so much time to spend with us. She stayed home with us for 10 years, from the time I was born, in 1969, to when my little sister started kindergarten in 1978. It was a traditional arrangement, and one both my parents believed in, and thought was in the best interests of the children. Once we were in school, she slowly reentered the workforce, eventually earning a master's degree and becoming a consultant.

It all sounds wonderful, does it not? Then, when I was 18 years of age, what happens to 50 percent of all families happened to us—my parents divorced. It was a reasonably amicable divorce, but life changed dramatically, none the less.

Fast-forward another 10 years. My father retired early at 55, while my mother continued to work. And then one day it hit me like a ton of bricks: My mother was going to have to work 10 years longer then my father. He was retired and enjoying life, but she was still getting up early every day and working 9 a.m. to 5 p.m. I couldn't help but notice that she had stayed home with us for a decade, and now was going to have to work an extra decade—in a sense, making up for this.

Is it fair? No. Is it common? Yes. My mom was caught in time, like so many other women. Is my father a bad guy? No. He's actually quite nice. They both just lived out a typical scenario of their generation—he worked hard to support us, and she stayed home caring for the children. And the unspoken deal was that my mom would always be provided for, as long as she stayed with my father. She could share in his retirement. They both assumed life would be this way. After all, no one plans to divorce.

I was angry. I would have given anything for my mom not to have to work. And I felt helpless. This anger and feeling of helplessness has fueled me in my work on underearning issues. I don't want this to happen to other women. Yes, it is wonderful to stay home and enjoy life with children. The distant future always feels so far off. But at 60 years old, many women long to retire, to enjoy their senior years, to work less and pursue other interests that have accumulated over a lifetime. There is no easy answer as to how to ensure that this happens. But part of the answer lies in being conscious.

According to the National Center for Women and Retirement Research, for every year a woman takes off to care for kids, it takes five years to catch up financially. I find myself groping for answers in the face of such a startling statistic. Do I value time spent with children? Absolutely. In my own life, I have chosen to work part-time for a while, in order to spend more time with my small son. But because I am so aware of these issues, I make sure that when I do work, I work hard, and am paid at the top of what I can command. I make sure I contribute the maximum to my retirement plan. And I think of the future as I map out my evolving career. I believe that if we do not lose sight of our financial lives we can take time off or work part time, to spend time with our children. But we must do it consciously and deliberately, while paying attention to money. Conscious decision making can take us a long way.

I would like to think that the Romance Myth is losing its grip on North American society, but at times it feels like it has just gone underground. Only a couple of generations ago (and some would argue that it continues still) there was a sense that a woman had a simple choice. She could choose freedom, or she could choose security. By choosing freedom, she was in essence choosing to always remain single. She might struggle financially and fear for her future, but the future was hers alone. Or she could choose security. And to choose security meant getting married. In marriage, she would be protected and provided for. It is easy to say that a woman should always choose "freedom," but until very recently, a woman had a very difficult time finding her own way in the business world and making enough money on her own to forge an independent life. And so, in the end, it did not really feel like a choice at all. "A woman has to eat!" was the practical refrain. So a woman usually kept up her end of the bargain and learned to cook, clean, raise children, and take care of her husband.

It's diffucult to get a sense of the history of the Romance Myth, because it's been the prevailing belief system for more than a millennia. Women's economic freedom is a relatively new phenomenon—a phenomenon that is not yet shared with many women in so many countries around the world. The Romance Myth has been fed to women from infancy, and many would argue that they are simply living out their programming. Parents looking out for their daughter's futures want their daughters to "marry well," while sons are educated to provide for themselves. This has changed only very recently. Judy, for example, came from a family of five—herself, her parents, and her two brothers. She spoke fondly of hardworking parents who wanted to do the right things for their children.

"I have no doubt that my parents loved me very much and did the best they could. They wanted to make sure I married a man 'above' their station, to have the life they never did. So they sent me to finishing school and tried to make sure I dated the right kind of boys. And for my brothers, they scrimped and saved to send them to college. It never occurred to any of us that I should go to college. It's hard to believe now."

Women have always been taken care of—first by their fathers, and then by their husbands. That's just how it's always been. Women were taught they were unable to rely on themselves for support, and that they must always depend on someone else. "Father knows best." "Listen to your husband." And as always, the payoff of this dependency was security.

It's possible we could have gone against the tide and focused on our career, but many women of today grew up with the unspoken message "A career is nice, but marriage and children are more important." With such training, is it any wonder so many women find it difficult to demand their fair share of the economic pie?

The Romance Myth is fundamentally a myth for women, not men. What message is sent to men? From an early age, men are taught that someday it will be up to them to provide for a family, and so, from an early age, they are oriented towards looking at work from a very practical point of view. They make sure they are paid as well as possible, for their future families will depend on them.

When I was in college, it was fashionable for those of us in the liberal arts programs to secretly look down on those in the business schools, those students who seemed to be in it just for the future financial payoff. And the majority of the business students were men. Yet how different would it be for the woman who is majoring in French Literature to know without a doubt that one day it will be up to her to support a family? Would she still have chosen to study French Literature? Imagine how different the world would be if women were as conscious of the importance of money and finance as men are, from an early age. Imagine how much more thoughtful they would be in their career decisions, how much more diligent they would be in their negotiating, and how much more carefully they would attend to their schooling, if they knew without a doubt that they would have to support a family one day.

Patricia Smith makes a fascinating point in her book *Each Of Us—How Every Woman Can Earn More in Corporate America* (Q1 Communicators, Inc., 1998); she comments that typically men see work as something they do *for* their family (emphasis here), while women often see work as something they do against their family's best interests. Women worry about the effect their working will have on their marriages and children. Men do not work with so clouded a conscience.

What complicates this is the different teaching boys and girls receive as children. Among the more potent and destructive ideas girls are taught is the importance of being a "good girl." Even today, many girls and women fall prey to the "Good Girl Syndrome." Simply put, the Good Girl Syndrome is a combination of needing to feel liked, while at the same time fearing making someone angry, or causing them displeasure.

Women are taught that if they follow the rules and work hard to please those around them, they will be rewarded. Judy remembered an incident from her days as a teenaged babysitter. A father of the young children she was charged with had made unreasonable requests of her. When she babysat, he told her she must wash all their dishes (which they left dirty for her), vacuum the house, bathe the children, and fold any clean laundry. Judy felt this was an absurd amount of work for the paltry sum she was paid, and complained to her mother about it. Her mother advised her to "be a good girl," and not say anything. She should do the extra work because she was lucky to have the job. If she complained, she might lose it. After two years of watching these children, she discovered by accident how much he paid the other babysitters he used. She was upset and resentful to learn that they made almost double what she did, but was still too afraid to ask for a raise.

When a woman fears displeasing someone, she certainly will not stick up for herself adequately in a job setting. In fact, falling prey to the Good Girl Syndrome keeps women from negotiating for their own best interests—be it a salary, a raise, or more benefits. Being a "good girl" can cause women to accept a smaller raise or slower advancement then they deserve. In effect, it causes women to undervalue their services.

With such training, women grow up fixated on the approval of their superiors, rather than the satisfaction that comes from earning at the top of their salary range. "Money talks," as the saying goes, yet women seem to be willing to accept praise and thanks in lieu of this money.

Unfortunately, it can be very difficult for a woman to override her programming to be "nice." She fears being labeled a "bitch," and no one wants to be that. Of course, we'd rather be liked. And yes, we all know there is a double standard. A man can demand changes and bark his orders, but when a woman engages in the same tactics, she can be seen as overly aggressive. In fact, it sometimes seems that any woman who acts like a man in business runs the risk of being labeled this negative word. But perhaps it is time for a woman to embrace her inner bitch, and use her to help accomplish financial goals. She can look out for a woman's own best interests without constantly being concerned about whether everyone else's needs are being met.

In the end, in order to avoid underearning, women must learn to adequately and appropriately gauge the worth of their skills and experience, and expect to be compensated appropriately. They cannot always be concerned with how their actions will appear to others. At its worst, a desire to please others can completely undermine a woman's ability to be adequately compensated for her work, so that she often ends up with only a pat on the back, and an empty bank account.

✎   **Exercise: Journal Questions**   ✐

Think back through your work history. Go all the way back to your first job. Do you see any evidence of the "Good Girl Syndrome" in action?

☞ Did I ever remain silent about a raise out of fear of rocking the boat?

☞ Did I ever do things I didn't want to, for fear of making a boss mad?

☞ Have I ever gone to great lengths to secure a boss's approval that resulted in praise, but no increased compensation?

Write down any incidences you can recall.

The Many Faces of Prince Charming

It can be very difficult for a woman to let go of the fantasy of the white knight swooping down to carry her off. Think of Cinderella. Did she not deserve to meet Prince Charming? After all, look at how hard she worked! Prince Charming was her ultimate reward for being a "good girl" and doing as she was told.

So just who is Prince Charming? Prince Charming is usually seen as a man—specifically, the man who will swoop down and carry the woman off to the castle, where she will never have to work again. Yet as I've worked with women on underearning, I've noticed that Prince Charming is not always a man, and when he is something else, he is harder to recognize, and therefore harder to overcome. Simply put, Prince Charming is anyone or anything a woman hopes will rescue her—that is, keep her from having to support herself. And as long as she harbors a secret desire for someone or something to take care of her, she will most likely never earn at her true potential.

One common form of Prince Charming is the idea or knowledge that a woman will be inheriting money someday, often from her parents. I've talked to women who believed they did not have to take retirement issues seriously, or worry about making good money, because when their parents died, they said, they would inherit enough so they didn't have to worry. Often times, when a woman is wrapped up in a financial fog, the knowledge of an inheritance can act like her ace in the hole. She never has to fully deal with money if she believes that, eventually, it will come to her with no effort at all on her part.

When I teach classes and seminars on underearning, I will often ask participants to brainstorm all the possible things Prince Charming could be. Their lists are quite remarkable. A popular Prince Charming is the lottery. If only they won the lottery, they could stop having to concentrate on this money thing. One woman saw her house appreciation as a form of Prince Charming.

"I know that in the back of my mind, I am counting on selling my house someday for a huge sum of money, and when I do, I will be okay. It helps me sleep at night—knowing that the house will take care of me, in a sense."

Others have said their children were a form of Prince Charming. That when they got older, they assumed their kids would care for them. Some argued welfare functioned as a form of Prince Charming. That as long as the government stepped in and provided, a woman wouldn't have the same incentive to go out there and earn good money. Other Prince Charmings were "the soaring stock market," "social security," and "pyramid schemes." One woman even said her husband's life insurance functioned as a Prince Charming failsafe. In case the real life Prince Charming ever died, his life insurance would continue to provide for her, and she wouldn't be forced to contend with making money.

Regardless of who your Prince Charming is, it is important to reflect on what in your life is enabling you to not take earning money seriously. Is there a secret part of your soul that is waiting for someone or something to take care of you? Are you waiting for someone to do it for you? Until you can honestly answer the question "Am I waiting for someone or something to rescue me?" it will be hard to overcome underearning.

✎ **Exercise: Journal Questions** ✎

The purpose of the following questions is to help you decide what could be operating as a "Prince Charming" in your life.

➥ Do I secretly long to win the lottery so I don't have to worry about money?

➥ Am I assuming I will inherit money and not have to worry about earning a lot?

➥ Am I waiting for a man to step in and take control of my finances, so I don't have to think about maximizing my earning power?

☞ In my heart, am I waiting for someone or
something to "do it for me?"

Write down as many Prince Charmings as you can
think of that may be operating in your life.

The Bag Lady

My 2-year-old son and I were walking hand-in-hand, making
our way home from the neighborhood park, when we came
upon an older woman who caught my eye. She was dressed in
clothes that at one time had been expensive and fashionable.
She did not seem crazy, nor was she trying to call attention to
herself. I might not even have noticed how old and frayed her
clothes were, were it not for the fact that she had taken the lid
off the garbage can and was carefully going through the contents,
adding some items to the many bags at her feet. Her eyes
darted furtively to my toddling son, who looked at her with
innocent eyes—no judgment, just curiosity on his small face.
She looked first at him, and then up at me, knowing he would
ask "the" question out loud, which of course he did.

"What she doing, Mommy?" he sputtered. He pulled at
my arm to slow down and watch her, and I tried to gently pull
on his arm to keep moving. I looked into her eyes and smiled,
and saw a mixture of defiance, embarrassment, and vacancy.

A few paces ahead out of her earshot, (I hoped), I replied,
"She's looking for something in the garbage can." It was a
straightforward answer to which my 2-year-old simply replied,
"Oh." But how much more complicated the reality was, and
how it pained my heart.

The "Bag Lady." The image of the proverbial bag lady, complete with her rusted shopping cart and bags of (to us) useless
odds and ends, evokes images of homelessness and feelings of
abandonment for all women. The fact that the bag lady has been
coined a "syndrome" means she has become the visible symbol
of women's greatest fear—that of having no one to care for them.

It is about more than desertion, or of going hungry. She evokes pity, disdain, and ridicule. She is about being ostracized, and she is a symbol of failure.

With so potent a symbol for what happens if the Romance Myth fails, is it any wonder so many women have nightmares about it? Like the Romance Myth, the Bag Lady Syndrome is based on a millennia of women's history. In the past, if a woman was not taken care of by someone, she could, quite literally, end up on the streets. As Susan Forward writes in *Money Demons* (Bantam, 1994), the Bag Lady Syndrome is deeply embedded in women's collective unconscious. "It reflects more then just the fear of financial ruin—it is the ultimate manifestation of all our fears about being alone, pitiable, disdained, and outcast." And to make matters worse, although most women know rationally that they are capable of making money to support themselves, another part of their psyche fears that they are in fact *not* capable. It is this part that calls to mind the images of the bag lady as we lie awake at night, wondering how we will support ourselves.

Unfortunately, there is a lot of truth behind the fears evoked by the bag lady. According to the Social Security Administration, only 37 percent of women older than age 62 receive social security benefits based solely on their own work records, and even those women receive only 76 percent as much as men. And because women spend more years out of the workforce, according to the US Census Bureau, they qualify for pensions only half as much as men. Compounding these statistics is the fact that women have saved only half the amount of personal savings as men their age. And according to the American Savings Education Council, 60 percent of women have never tried to figure out how much money they need to save for retirement, and 40 percent have not even saved for retirement period! Add to this that as of the year 2000, women live seven years longer then men, and you can see the disaster looming.

It is not that all the women in these statistics will end up on the streets. However, it means these women can never stop working. But don't most women have images of their "golden years," and the many dreams and hobbies they hope to pursue? While it is true that the definition of retirement has changed quite dramatically (most of us do not want to retire full-time to the golf course), when I ask women what retirement means to them, they invariably respond with something like, "It means having the freedom to do whatever I want." Being obliged to work forever is not freedom.

And it gets worse. A 1998 study by the National Center for Women and Retirement Research found that among women age 35 to 55, 1/2 to 2/3 will be impoverished by the age of 70. That means that for every 100 women, 50 to 66 of them will have to continue working indefinitely, or live in poverty.

While these statistics are painful, I do not share them to depress you. Depression only leads to more inaction. I share them to help shake women out of their denial that everything is okay. That they can continue on as they always have. No! If women do not take control of their earning power, the future will not be theirs to shape. I cherish freedom above almost all other values, and it pains me greatly to see the loss of freedom these statistics mean to so many women. But that loss of freedom does not have to happen.

When a woman believes in Prince Charming, she never takes control of her career in the way she should. With the image of Bag Lady, she has a feeling of futility, of being paralyzed, of watching things come to pass that are beyond her control. It is this sense of being powerless that is so terrifying. That at any moment, the fates may align and she will be thrown out on the streets with the empty shopping bags waiting to be filled with other people's castoffs.

✎ **Exercise: Journal Questions** ✐

➡ What is the specific image I have in my mind of the Bag Lady? What do I see?

➡ What does she represent to me, personally?

➡ When is the first time I remember thinking about or fearing the Bag Lady?

The dream of being carried off by Prince Charming is a mirror reflection of becoming the Bag Lady. If one does not happen, women become the other. But what truly unites Prince Charming to the Bag Lady is the issue of inaction. With both, women are the passive watchers of their fate, hoping beyond hope that someone (or something) will rescue her, and fearful that someone won't. If she is lucky, she will live in a nice house. If she is unlucky, the streets are her home. In both worlds, women do not take control of their fate. The antidote, therefore, lies in taking action.

Anger and Responsibility

Yet it is not so easy. Anger overwhelms many women. Yes, they have been deceived. And I believe it is the baby boomer women who've been cheated the most. They are the generation that is caught in a difficult time. For their generation, more than for any other, the message they were given started as one thing, and then switched to another. Many boomer women were brought up under the Romance Myth. It is what they were taught, and what they were groomed for. And yet half way through their lives, somehow the rules changed.

It is doubly ironic that this changing of the rules may have been their own doing. It is these women who have fought so valiantly for women's rights—the right to choose, the right to earn, the right to lead life as they see fit. The problem is that when women are given rights, then by necessity, they are also given responsibility. And it is this responsibility that can suddenly seem so scary.

"I was out there marching in the 1970s, with everyone else," said Judy. "I still have my buttons: Equal Pay for Equal Work. Of course I've believed in and fought for women's rights. But I guess I never thought of the reverse side—how hard it would be to live this new life. I wanted to earn equally to men, but that meant I had to go out there and market myself, and raise my prices. It was easier to just keep doing the same thing, and hope things worked out."

"Hoping for things to work out" is not about taking control and responsibility. When a woman shirks responsibility, she becomes dependent, and loses her freedom. And what is the opposite of freedom? It is restriction and dependency. As Collette Dowling says in *Maxing Out,* "Dependency is at the heart of women's difficulty in creating security for themselves. As long as a part of us is involved in the idea of romantic rescue, we will continue jeopardizing our financial independence." If a woman does not know in her heart that she is capable of taking care of herself financially, she can never feel fully autonomous.

And there is a bigger problem. The Romance Myth is a fraud. Period. The Romance Myth, while it may be quite appealing, is simply no longer true. Eighty percent of American women will, at one time or another in their lives, become wholly responsible for their own financial welfare, whether they like it or not, and whether or not they are prepared. And perhaps more startling is Collette Dowling's assertion that women who never marry actually are better off financially than women who do! This is due to the high divorce rate, and the likelihood of outliving your husband if you do stay married. According to the General Accounting Office, 80 percent of widows now in poverty were not poor before their husbands died. And the average age of widows, in 2000, is 55! Complicating this is that not infrequently, women in marriages hand over the reigns of finance to their husbands, so once they are alone (90 percent of women end up alone, due to never marrying, divorce, and widowhood), they do not feel capable of managing their financial lives.

Now please don't misunderstand me. I am not saying marriage is bad. I am quite fond of my own husband. But marriage can lure women into a false sense of security, and keep them from taking charge of their earning power and finances. Sometimes it seems as if married women feel they have a "get out of jail free" card. That if you are married, you do not have to worry about these issues. Wrong. First of all, it is no longer fair to assume our husbands will always work to provide for us. Ideally, spouses should see themselves as a team. And though no one wants to think about it, more than half of all married couples end up divorced. It is wrong to assume you don't have to worry about money. In fact, I would say it is irresponsible and dangerous. You need to know that no matter what, you will be okay. There is nothing that beats this feeling.

In spite of women's dawning suspicions that Prince Charming might not be coming, that they may lose their Prince Charming, or that the current Prince Charming may not be all that he was cracked up to be, they persist in holding on to the myth. Why? Many women lack the confidence that they can take charge of their financial destinies, even though they know they must. The system *is* stacked against women, who can alternate between being angry at the state of the world, with feeling overwhelmed and incapable of taking over their financial futures. Because of the discrimination that women have experienced, it is no wonder that so many have no confidence in their own abilities to make it on their own.

And even though women strive to change, it can feel difficult to keep up with the changing role of women. Women have lived through the collision of two worldviews—the world of being wife, mother, and homemaker; and the world where they are expected to be economically self-sufficient. Many women are doing their best to reconcile these two worldviews in their lives. They seem to be working harder to keep up with it all, and it is easy to assume that making more money would require yet more hard work. But as a woman overcomes under-earning, she may find that she only needs to work smarter, not harder.

I believe that many women are angry that they've ended up alone. This is not how it was supposed to be! And they are overwhelmed at managing money, partially because they believe they are not capable of managing it, and partially because they can't let go of the fantasy that someone will be there to help them, or to do it for them. And so, they go on waiting, and continue to be passive.

When a woman takes control of her finances, it has a dramatic effect on her self-esteem, and this new self-esteem helps women truly feel financial peace and freedom. Without self-created financial stability, it is virtually impossible to experience true freedom. And what is true freedom? It is autonomy, self-determination, and independence. It is choice, and it is freewill. And it is this deep sense of freedom that gives a woman peace and inner security.

Notice that I said "self-created financial stability." It is not about becoming enormously wealthy, or having as much money as humanly possible. It is to know that you are okay—that all your needs are met, and you have the resources both to enjoy life, and to save for the future. Your goal is to have enough, and to have the peace of mind that comes with knowing that when push comes to shove, you can indeed take care of yourself. (We define just how much "enough" is in Chapter 6.)

In the end, money means freedom, and money means power. Traditionally, women have shied away from money as power. But it is with this power that the insidious hold of Prince Charming can be broken, once and for all. With this power, you can finally become mistress of your own fate.

Chapter Four

When Underearning Serves Us

Kristine, an architect for a small firm in the city, was 29 years old, single, overworked, and stressed out. Tired of struggling financially, she came in to see me, citing very typical financial counseling reasons. She was tired of being in debt, suspected her spending may be a little out of control, and felt like she could never really get ahead, despite how much she worked.

For several months we worked on her personal finances. We started with creating a personalized spending plan so we could see what was really happening, and she could decide where she wanted her money to go each month. We then took a hard look at her debt and developed a reasonable debt reduction plan. She began to save money and for the first time, felt like she was starting to get ahead.

About four months into our process, Kristine began to see that she just wasn't making enough money. She was tired of trying to balance her personal monthly spending plan with the amount of money she made, and began to talk about earning more. I've noticed that many times people assume the answer to their financial issues is either to get out of debt, or to spend less money. While both of these may be valid solutions, sometimes the real problem is that the person is not making enough money in the first place. If this is the case, they will perpetually fall behind, no matter how little money they spend. Kristine might do okay if she carefully watched her money, but it seemed obvious that she would benefit from earning more. She was still working for the same firm she started with out of college, so a move to a new firm would most certainly have meant more money.

However, like many people, Kristine was comfortable where she was. No, she wasn't happy, but she was overwhelmed by the change a move would imply. She went back and forth on whether she was willing to put herself out there and try to earn more. But as she continued in her process and kept looking at her numbers, she finally decided she would like to make more money. The way she talked, she seemed to almost be convincing herself of this. "Of course I would like to make more money. Who wouldn't?" So she decided to prepare her resume and start doing some interviewing with other firms.

Each session after that, I asked Kristine how the job hunting process was going. "Fine," was the standard reply, but when I pressed for details, none were forthcoming. I began to ask more detailed questions, and it became obvious that Kristine was not taking any action. Yet she kept saying she would, but each time she came back to a session, still nothing had happened.

Finally, one day during one of our financial counseling sessions, I put the question to Kristine in a different way.

"Kristine, let's pretend that I can wave my magic money wand over you and give you a new job overnight that pays more than $100,000 a year. What would happen? How would your life be different? What would you have to do?"

And then I sat for a long time in silence. You learn to respect silence in counseling settings, and so I waited, for it seemed something was forthcoming. At long last, she said, "I'd have to deal with my parents."

Then there followed another long pause. When she said nothing else, I asked her, "Tell me about this. How would you have to deal with your parents?"

"I'd have to support them," she replied after another long pause.

I knew a little of Kristine's past, from some previous sessions and our initial intake. Kristine was the only child of older parents. They were almost 40 years old when they had her, and unfortunately, they were not good parents. They had abused Kristine her whole life—sometimes physically, always emotionally. Kristine had already done a great deal of therapy dealing with this, and she was in a good place. Her emotional wounds felt healed and she had gotten on with her life. Still, she did not like her parents, and this was understandable. The problem was that somewhere along the line, she had received a message that it was up to her to take care of her parents in their old age.

Kristine remembered a Christmas party when she was 16 years of age, her aunt told her, "Krissy, it's all up to you, you know. You better make sure you make good money someday, because you're going to have to take care of your parents. That's your job...."

Indeed, Kristine had received the message loud and clear that it was up to her to take care of them. And now they were older, in poor health, and financially unprepared for their retirement years. She felt that they were looking to her for support, but Kristine did not want to give her parents any money. She did not like them, and yet despite years of therapy, she felt it wasn't okay to feel this way. A part of her wanted to say, "Fend for yourself! I'm not going to help you!" Yet she felt she couldn't say this, for they were her parents, and so she created her life in such a way that it was a moot point. She made sure she carried enough debt and never truly made "enough" money, so there was no extra money to support them. In essence, her underearning was serving her.

As much as some women say they want to stop underearning, they continue to underearn because it is somehow serving them. Though this is a difficult notion to look at, it is crucial to examine this aspect of underearning. So far, I've explored two of the reasons women may be underearning: They may feel there is some perceived virtue in not having money, or they may secretly be waiting for someone take care of them. But sometimes, women will continually hamstring themselves to avoid earning money because their underearning is *benefiting* them in some way.

Actually, it can be said that all underearning has some benefit. When we fall into noble poverty, our underearning allows us to claim a certain sense of moral superiority, even though the true culprit may be low self-esteem. And certainly, the Romance Myth serves to keep the space open for our would-be rescuer, despite the detrimental effect this "waiting" has on our lives. So it can be said that when anyone underearns, this behavior is in some way self-serving, or else they would not engage in it. (Of course most of this happens unconsciously, which makes it far more difficult to detect.) But there are some "forms" of underearning that are even less noticed than noble poverty or falling into the Romance Myth. These examples of underearning are harder to classify. What unites them is that at the root of all of them is a desire to keep things the way they are. Life becomes structured around maintaining a certain "status quo." This "self-serving underearning," as I will call it, always has a benefit. Hence, a part of us does not want to overcome it. We become conflicted over making more money. A part of us would like to earn more and a part of us wants things to stay the same.

Self-serving underearning is fraught with paradox. On the one hand we say we want to earn more, and we try desperately to do so. But if our underearning is in some way benefiting us, then no matter how hard we try to earn more, we will always sabotage our own best efforts, often to our own frustration. We will either sabotage ourselves by some action that actively causes us to lose money, or we simply will do nothing. Because of this, true self-serving underearning can be very difficult to overcome.

Common Motivations Behind Underearning

In this chapter, we will be looking at some examples and stories of when underearning serves people in some way. This is not meant to be a definitive list of the ways underearning might be benefiting someone. There would be as many ways on that list as there are people. But it is my hope that if you look at several different reasons underearning commonly serves another person, you will be better able to look into your own life to see if you, too, might be doing the same thing. Often, it is in reading someone else's story that we recognize our own. But remember, there are no tidy definitions or classifications of how underearning serves women. People are complex, and their reasons and motivations tend to be multifaceted. As you read through these, see if any speak to you. Are there any that have some aspect with which you identify?

To Stay in Our Comfort Zone

"I realized that if I continue to underearn, I can stay in my comfort zone. I won't have to do anything different. I am afraid to take risks."

"If I underearn, I can stay where I am and continue being a workaholic. It's what I know, what I am familiar with."

"I know I don't make enough. But if I want to make more, I might have to leave my job, and that overwhelms me. This way, everything stays the same. At least I know what to expect."

I always ask women at my underearning seminars how underearning might be serving them. What is the benefit? I receive all kinds of answers. Not uncommon is the benefit of keeping everything the same. If things stay the same, there is no risk or chance of loss.

Underearning benefits you by allowing you to protect yourself. If you really put yourself out there, you run the risk of rejection. Most underearners would rather do anything than risk rejection, even if that means doing nothing. So underearning serves to keep one right where one is—safe and sound, and probably poor.

Underearning allows people to keep things the same. You don't risk losing anything that making more money might take away. I remember one woman telling me that if she earned more money, she might lose her friends.

"None of us make a lot of money. It's like this common bond we all share. Sure, we complain about not having money all the time, but we're all in the same boat. If I suddenly made a lot of money, I could lose my friends. Of course they would say they were happy for me, but there would be a wall between us. It just wouldn't be the same anymore."

Deep down, would you rather things stay the same? Do you long for the tried and true, the familiar and comfortable? Are you afraid that making more money might take you out of your comfort zone?

To Avoid a Future Event

As we saw with Kristine, sometimes women underearn because, otherwise, something would come to pass in the future that they want to prevent from happening.

My friend Maggie has a sister who is mentally disabled. This sister had two children by a man who later died. Her sister was not really capable of taking care of these children on her own, so she moved in with their mother, who helped her raise them. Maggie's mom has a long-term chronic illness and does not expect to be around in another 10 years, but she does her best in raising these two grandchildren.

Maggie is the oldest in the family and is seen as the "responsible one." Yet she has never made a lot of money. She is very capable and smart, but has always opted for low paying jobs. One day when we were talking, she wondered out loud the real reasons behind her low income.

"I know that they expect me to be the guardian of my niece and nephew someday. It's not like I don't love them. They are great kids. But I really like my life. I like living alone and doing all the things I enjoy. I guess the truth is that I don't want to be saddled with two children. It would change everything. But as long as I make so little, it doesn't really seem to be an option—me taking them. I mean, I'd have to make decent money if I was going to take two kids in, wouldn't I?"

The questions you have to ask yourself are: Is there something that would happen if I made a lot of money that I would like to avoid? What would happen in my life if suddenly I earned double what I currently make? Would there be any new expectations put on me?

Because We Fear Giving Something up

Remember Teresa, the therapist who assumed that professionals who charge a lot of money must be unscrupulous somehow? She resisted raising her rates, supposedly because of this belief. However, evidence of her underearning was everywhere. She always turned a blind eye to opportunity. When her friends told her about that new possible job opening at a mental health clinic, she never even bothered to inquire about it, even though she kept saying she wanted to make more money. As you will see, one of the symptoms of being a "self-serving underearner" is saying you are going to take some action, but never doing anything. I suspected Teresa's underearning was indeed serving her, for she rarely took action towards making more money, even though opportunities consistently presented themselves.

"Oh, it probably wouldn't pay enough money." "I've heard that she is just awful to work for." "I bet they would demand I put in too many hours. It just isn't worth it."

Maybe. Maybe not. She never inquired.

I asked Teresa one day what was the one thing she was most afraid she would have to give up, if she got a job that paid a lot of money. Without missing a beat, she said, "freedom." She went on to say, "I value my free time tremendously. I've always spent a lot of time with my kids, because I felt it was important. And now I have hobbies and a lot of friends. Life just doesn't seem worth living if you don't have time to do the things you love."

"Do you assume that a job that paid a lot would take all your time?"

"Absolutely."

So there it was. If she valued her free time, and assumed any good paying job would take it, why would she pursue a job that paid a lot of money? She could say she wished she made more money all she wanted, but did she really wish for this? Deep down, she felt these two desires—freedom and money—were mutually exclusive.

In fact, most underearners believe that making enough money comes at too high a cost. Barbara Stanny, in her book *Secrets of Six Figure Women* (Harper Collins, 2002), points out that women who are high earners usually think in terms of reasonable "trade-offs"—would I be willing to give up x if I got y? But underearners think only in terms of sacrifice. It is all about giving up something too important to lose. When a part of you assumes you will always have to make a great sacrifice when it comes to higher salaries, you may sabotage your own efforts. On the surface, you will claim to want more money. But if a great sacrifice will have to occur, maybe you don't really want that to happen after all.

For mothers, this can feel especially difficult. Sometimes when we fear we would have to give up a lot of time, we worry how this will affect our children, or how it would reflect on us as mothers. I know many women who assume a high paying position would leave little time for their families, even though they may currently be exhausting themselves trying to make ends meet.

All of this would have made more sense if Teresa had not already been a very busy woman. Like so many underearners, she actually worked very hard, but did not make a lot for all her trouble. She was consistently "underemployed" and was always looking for extra work on the side. She had her own small private practice, which never quite earned enough, so she also worked part time for the community hospital in their out-patient treatment programs. For more money, she would run therapy groups at night or on the weekend. Then she spent a lot of her time going from one place to the next. Unfortunately, two part-time jobs can equal more then one full-time job, with all the logistics of coming and going. Yet she resisted looking for one primary position that could replace these jobs.

What do you assume you would have to "sacrifice" or give up, in order to make more money? Is this really true? Would you really lose something? And if you would, is it possible that the payoff could be worth it?

For Fear the Money Would Be Taken Away

"I worry that if I made more money, it would just get taken away." I've heard many variations on this concern, but what fascinates me is what is often underneath it. Many women I know actually fear that if they made more money, they would feel pressured into *giving* their money away, usually to aging parents, as we saw with Kristine, or to dependents who never seem fully capable of taking care of themselves financially as adults.

Eleanor, who you got to know in the noble poverty chapter, often struggled with giving her daughter money. Even though she knew she didn't have enough to "loan" her each month (she rarely paid her back), she couldn't help herself. She felt guilty that her daughter wasn't able to take care of herself. She felt it must have been some fault in how she raised her that she has been unable to consistently pay her bills and stay employed in her 20s. So inevitably, when she comes around asking for money, Eleanor gives it to her, and then later worries how she will pay her own bills.

"I just know that if I were suddenly making a lot of money, I would end up giving a ton of money to Michelle. How could I say no to her, if she needed it, and I had it? So what's the point of making a lot of money? It would just end up going to her, and I know that that's not good for her, but I know I can't help it. She's my daughter!"

One of the problems with giving money to our adult children is that we are sending the message to them that we do not believe they can take care of themselves. It is part of the responsibility of parents to give their children the internal knowledge that they really can take care of themselves and make their way in the world. When we consistently bail them out, we are sending a message that they are not capable after all. And sometimes, when parents give their adult children money, it can be because the parent wants to still feel needed, and maintain a certain connection to the child. Unfortunately, this financial connection is seldom healthy.

Whether we worry we would feel pressure to give money to our adult children, our aging parents, or our down-and-out siblings, this knowledge can seriously dampen our desire and drive to move forward and take care of ourselves financially. I've had some clients deal with this by not letting their relatives know how much they really make. While this means fostering secrecy around money, if it is for your own protection, sometimes it is necessary.

Underearners often talk as if they have no choice in the matter. They assume it is not all up to them—that they must do what others ask of them—so if someone asks for money, they must hand it over. There is this fundamental feeling that they are not in control of their life or their resources. When you don't feel in control, sometimes it is easier to make sure you have nothing that can be taken away from you.

If you suddenly made a lot more money, do you think you would feel pressured into giving a portion of it away? Do you think your money might get taken away? If so, does this make you less likely to try to increase your income?

Because We Worry We Wouldn't Be Able to Handle the Money

Judy, our special events planner, voiced her concern she wouldn't be able to deal with a lot of money if it did come to her. "What if I mess it up?" she asked. During her marriage, her husband had overseen their investments. But it was Judy who did the day-to-day handling of their money, and she was actually quite competent. She kept a balanced checkbook and was very sensible when it came to household budgeting. But because Judy was uninvolved with their stock portfolios and retirement accounts, she assumed that investing was something she just couldn't understand, and would undoubtedly mess up.

When it comes to looking at our big-picture financially, I've noticed that many women act as if they are paralyzed. These women may be smart and quite competent professionally. They may even handle other people's money quite well. But when it comes to their own investments, they freeze up. They are overwhelmed at everything they do not know and they don't know where to begin, so they do nothing.

When you make very little money, these issues stay in the background. What is the point of learning how to deal effectively with money, when you feel as if you are living paycheck to paycheck? Investing is a moot point when you are struggling just to pay your bills. But what if you suddenly started making a lot more money? You would be forced to look at the big financial picture, and this terrifies many women. It may be easier to go on living hand-to-mouth. We know how to survive, because we are survivors. But do we know how to thrive?

So ask yourself, does your concern over learning how to handle a greater amount of money play a part in your self-sabotage over landing a higher paying job or asking for a raise?

To Punish Someone

Although it sounds hard to believe, there are times when women underearn in order to punish someone else. I once had a client who was a registered nurse. She was quite competent and liked her work. She came into financial counseling for typical reasons. She carried a large amount of credit card debt and was always stressed out financially. And at 37 years old, she had moved back home to live with her mom and dad. She said she felt she had no choice. With her debt, and not making enough money, there was no way she could live on her own. But she told me she that she hated living with her parents. They treated her like a child, and not the adult woman she was. But when I suggested that she might want to move back out, she balked.

"How do you expect me to rent an apartment in the city on what I make? Maybe if I made more, but even so, it would be impossible with the rents they charge these days!"

When we went over her work history, it was full of jobs she had stayed in for very short periods of time, jobs she never should have had in the first place, and jobs that she hated and then quit. It was a fascinating pattern that had led her back to living with her parents in her late 30s, and one that smacked of self-sabotage. But there was always a reason, always an excuse, as to why each job had turned out like it did.

She started therapy about the same time she started financial counseling, and between the two, she began processing her feelings and motivations. One day she commented, "You know, I don't think my parents were such good parents, when I was growing up. I used to not be able to say that, but it's true! They never supported me in anything I did. And when I wanted to go off to college, not only would they not support my decision, they wouldn't help me pay for it, even though I know they had the money!"

I ventured a comment. "Do you think that living with them now is somehow getting back at them for not supporting you before? After all, they are supporting you now."

"Of course they are supporting me now, though they sure don't make it easy! They can't throw me out in the street, you know. They had to take me in."

"It sounds to me like maybe you're getting even with them for not taking care of you like they should have when you were growing up. And you've told me numerous times how hard it was to get through college, having to work and pay for it yourself. By your not making a lot of money, they are forced to take care of you and pay you back for this, in a sense."

There was a long pause while she pondered this. Finally, she said, "I never thought of it that way, but I think there is some truth in that. I always talk about how they 'owe' me for all the things they did and didn't do. I guess I am making them 'pay,' in a way...."

There can be many ways women punish the people around them by underearning. Tina, our artist, told me once that a part of her was glad she didn't make a lot of money. If she made more money, her ex could cut down on the amount of alimony he was currently paying. She was still so angry over the divorce, she was glad he was forced to pay such a large amount.

Does your continued underearning affect the people around you? Are you hurting someone by your continued underearning, and is a part of you glad for this?

Because a Dream Was Crushed in Our Past

Sometimes, people underearn to keep themselves from thinking about opportunities lost to them and dreams that were deferred. As you will see when I talk about maintaining the status quo, underearning helps keep you where you are. It keeps one occupied and busy. When something traumatic has happened to someone, the last thing they want is to have the time to dream and think, because to their unconscious mind, certain aspects of life are already over. Why dwell on the possibilities of the future when your past dreams have already been crushed? Maybe this is as good as it gets, so we should just knuckle down and do our best. Keeping your eyes down and avoiding thinking too deeply about things keeps the pain of the past at bay.

When Mary, the administrative assistant, was 6 years old, she wanted to be a veterinarian more than anything else in the world. This dream stayed with her as she grew. As a girl, she was the child who secretly brought home the wounded animals—secretly, because her parents would allow no animals in the house. She longed to have a dog, a cat, a bird, a hamster—you name it. "Too messy and too expensive," was the standard reply.

When she was eight years old, Mary found a small sparrow with a wounded leg. She carefully picked it up and brought it home, making it a cozy home in a shoebox that she kept under her bed. She used the little money she received from the neighbor for doing some chores to go to the pet store and buy special bird food. For almost three weeks, she cared for this sparrow with no one knowing. Then one day, when her mother was in her room, the tiny bird began chirping, and was discovered by her mom.

"Just who do you think you are? You can't possibly take care of any animal, let alone a wounded bird!"

Mary received a prompt spanking and was put on restriction for three weeks. Her mother took the sparrow, and vanished with it. The words, *Just who do you think you are?* echoed in her mind.

Mary's dream of being a veterinarian stayed with her. But college was not in the picture. Mary's home was full of poverty, and warmth did not exude from its walls. Her self-esteem took a beating from the very beginning. She never really believed in herself, and didn't know anyone who believed in her either. She was one of many children, and her parents seldom had time for her. When they did, no encouraging words were offered.

When Mary was in high school and finally ventured to ask about college, she received this reply: "Just who do you think you are, Miss Smarty? First of all, where would we get the money, and second, it would be a waste if we did, because you would never get into college! Get sensible. If you are lucky, you'll graduate from high school and get an office job, like the other girls."

So Mary graduated, and got an office job, like the other girls. Now age 39, married with two children, she was profoundly unhappy. She did not enjoy what she was doing and knew she was not earning enough money. Yet, she certainly had never asked for a raise or looked for a better job. Why bother? Just who did she think she was, anyway?

Mary's underearning was serving to keep her busy and occupied. With little money and no time for anything, she didn't have time to think of the future, the future lived without her dream. Why would she want to think of the future? It was bleak. Once some women give up on their dreams, they create their finances in such a way that it ensures they can't follow their dreams, and therefore it is not their fault that they don't.

"See? I don't make enough money to go back to school." By underearning and locking themselves into a small life (through not having enough money or time), they nail a lid into the coffin they'd rather not be reminded of.

Because We are Really Living Someone Else's Dream

When LaDonna was growing up, her father talked constantly about the big world of business, and his own trade of advertising. Yes, sir, if you knew anything about sales and marketing, you could rule the world! LaDonna listened to him talk, but possessed little enthusiasm for business. Instead, she buried herself in books and traveled to far off places in her imagination. When she was in college, she declared English as her major, but

when she told her father, he had a fit. English?! What good was that
for business? Major in Business Administration! LaDonna resisted for a while, but felt he must be right, so she studied business.
Later, she toyed with different graduate programs for a while,
but then ended up pursuing an MBA as well. Now, in her 40s,
she makes "decent" money. Some would not see LaDonna as
an underearner at all, but remember that underearning is very
relative.

LaDonna always felt stressed out financially. No matter
how much she and her husband made, she always felt they
were living paycheck to paycheck. They wracked up enormous
credit card debt as well. Her father, who bailed them out from
time to time, was always baffled as to why his daughter was
not doing better financially. At this stage in her career, she
should have been making well over $100,000. But not only was
she not an effective negotiator, on her own behalf, she didn't
really seem motivated to move up the corporate ladder.

When LaDonna turned 45, she felt she entered a mid-life
crisis. It hit her that she was living someone else's dream for
her—her father's dream. She realized her life had been shaped
by someone else, not herself. She was not even sure she knew
what her own dreams were, it had been so many years since she
thought about them. The door to the exciting future she had
envisioned as a child felt like it closed a long time ago.

Her underearning had served to keep her from thinking
about and realizing this. Because she felt she had no choice but
to follow her father's recommendations all those years, she
had put her head down and worked without thinking. She kept
herself busy and occupied so she didn't have time to contemplate the sad fact that she wasn't living her own dream, but
someone else's. Her work did not come from a place of passion
or vision. At the same time, her underearning served to punish
her father. By not making enough money, she forced him to
bail her out, all the while resenting where she was in her life,
because of him.

To Maintain the Status Quo

Women will always find ways to continue underearning if it is to their advantage in some way, and one of the best ways to continue underearning is to maintain the status quo. You simply do nothing. When you don't really want things to change, for whatever the reason, you will inevitably structure your life to keep from moving forward. You will subtly hamstring any efforts you make to create positive change. People usually use passive underearning to accomplish this, which makes it doubly hard to see. They can say, "See, I'm not doing anything to hamper myself. Things just aren't working out." And they are correct—they are not doing anything.

If you never really make enough money, then you can't pursue different plans and dreams. Ideas become irrelevant, because you don't have the resources to see them through to fruition. Life just goes along, the same as it always has been. And sometimes, people operate from a belief system that it just isn't possible to have the life they want. Many underearners assume that it's just not possible to live their dreams. And if that is their core belief, it is very difficult to imagine a different ending to the story of life you are writing. And as much as you may not like your life, it is familiar. It can be too stressful to think about following a different course. It is always easier to remain the same, regardless of how painful the present may be.

How do women maintain the status quo? One of the most effective ways to ensure nothing will change is to make sure you have no time to do anything. Of course usually people try hard to create the illusion that they are trying to change. They give lip service to wanting to make more money, often for the benefit of those around them. A part of them even believes they do want to earn more. But then there is no action to back up these words.

Underearners who engage in self-serving underearning are notorious for having no time. This is part of maintaining the status quo. They keep themselves busy so as to have no time to attend to deeper issues, or actually make progress towards goals. They engage in endless activities, and sometimes, they just fritter their time away. Time is one of our most precious resources, and if you don't really want to do something, simply make sure you have no time in which to do it. Self-serving underearners make sure they have no time, and then use not having time as their primary excuse as to why they are not taking any action. Interestingly, those underearners wrapped up in noble poverty say they can't pursue their dreams or goals because they have no money. The self-serving underearners usually say they have no time.

Remember Teresa, the therapist, who feared giving up her freedom? She kept herself enormously busy, going from one job to the next, spending time with friends, and on hobbies. She made sure there was no time to look at these deeper issues and tackle her underearning.

Judy, our special events planner, gave her time away in droves. One of the ways she underearned, in fact, was by volunteering her time too much. She gave herself away—her time, skills, expertise—for no money. This contributed to her underearning in several ways. First, she worked a great deal without being paid. Second, she tired herself out so she didn't really have the energy to focus on making more money. For example, she knew she needed to market more to build up her business, but there was no time in which to do this. She made sure of that.

Eleanor, who worked for the nonprofit, spent all her free time working for various other causes she felt strongly about. And when she wasn't working or volunteering, she was reading to relax, or should I say, escape. She could read a novel a night. She made sure she never had to dwell on these issues, or actually make changes in her life.

The question we have to ask ourselves is this: *Am I so busy that I can't change, or do I not want to change, so I keep myself busy?*

Self-serving underearners have wishes, not goals. They "wish" things would change (supposedly), but never really do anything about it. I once heard the word goal defined as "dreams with deadlines." Deadlines keep us moving and on target. Most underearners do not work with deadlines, because deadlines get us to our goals.

As Julia Cameron writes about in *Money Drunk, Money Sober* (Ballantine Wellspring, 1992), people wrapped up in maintaining the status-quo (she calls them "money maintainers"), constantly say "I'm going to," and then take no action towards the goal. Of course, they always have a litany of excuses. And as we know, not having any time is usually at the top.

It's important to add that for many underearners, what they really lack is vision. It is not possible to really have goals unless one has vision first. Underearners, who tend to keep themselves and their lives restricted, find it difficult to feel expansive and to live expansively. They have great difficulties seeing the greater possibilities of their lives. And because they lack a vision for the life they want, they continue on as they always have, despite the pain. So ask yourself—can you envision a different story for your life, or can you envision a happier ending, to the story you are living?

Processing Our Emotions and Taking Action

It is imperative for these underearners to get in touch with their emotions. Self-serving underearners spend a lot of time trying not to think and feel, but if they truly want to end underearning, they must look within themselves and let their feelings rise to the surface. It can be very painful as women become aware of their anger, resentments, regrets, and uncertainties. They've been telling themselves that everything is just fine for so long, that when they really start to look, they can be overwhelmed by a tidal wave of repressed emotions. Sometimes, it is helpful to use a therapist in this phase. It can be scary when one confronts years of unacknowledged emotions.

When self-serving underearners "wake-up" and begin to process their underearning, they can feel angry and robbed. They suddenly realize their fear has robbed them of a chance to have a better life, and it can feel like it's too late now. It is as if they suddenly see what they have been doing, and become angry with themselves for all the opportunities they've let pass by. This is a lot to process. As we've seen, a lifetime of underearning does have dire consequences for our later lives. The money lost compounds over time to a staggering amount. This can feel overwhelming, both in the magnitude of the task ahead and in coping with the anger and resentment about what has happened.

But it is important to realize that it is never too late to improve your situation. Women need to believe, deep down, that they can take control right now, and improve their lives! A defeatist attitude will get them nowhere. Conquering underearning now, and not in 10 years, will make an enormous difference to one's quality of life in years to come. And the most effective way to overcome regret about the past is to actively work to safeguard the future.

Chapter Five

The Money Fog

"How is it possible that we're living paycheck to paycheck with the kind of money we make? I make more than $60,000 a year! That should be more than enough!"

LaDonna, a corporate accounts executive, was pacing around my office during her first appointment.

"Sometimes I think I wouldn't have financial problems if I just made more money, but it seems like no matter how much we make, we always end up in debt! It's not that I mind having debt. After all, everyone has credit card debt. But it's getting overwhelming. I just got a raise a few months ago, so I won't see another one for a while. And we can't seem to make anything more than the minimum payments. With the interest they charge, I'm getting scared that we'll never be able to pay it off."

Eventually, LaDonna calmed down enough to sit down and talk with me about the current state of her finances. She and her husband both worked hard, and earned good salaries. Like many professional people, they didn't feel they had to watch every penny, and tended to spend as they pleased. But debt has a habit of creeping up on you, as it had on LaDonna. After not paying attention to what was happening, it was a rude awakening for her to realize that they owed more than $60,000 in credit card debt alone.

"Truthfully, I'm not really sure how much we owe. I'm afraid to add it up. But I think it's got to be around $60,000. Do you realize that's my annual salary?"

LaDonna is describing a financial state of being that is unfortunately common to many people. Many women are stressed out about how much they owe in debt, and many more are not even sure how much they owe. Nor are they sure where their money is going. These women are living in what is called "the money fog"—a form of *self-induced vagueness over money*. This vagueness has a profound impact on our lives and plays a crucial role in our underearning.

✎   **Exercise: The Money Fog**   ✐

Take a moment and answer yes or no to the following questions, to determine how thick your money fog is:

- ➠ Are you clear about the total amount of money you owe on credit cards and other debts?

- ➠ Do you regularly balance a checkbook?

- ➠ Do you follow a budget or spending plan, each month?

- ➠ Do you know where all your money goes?

- ➠ Do you know the amount of money you need each month to live comfortably?

- ➠ If you are self-employed, do you know exactly how much you are making each month?

- ➠ Are you in control of your cash? (Have you ever been perplexed when you run through cash faster than you thought you would? "I just went to the ATM yesterday!")

☞ Do you know if you are saving enough for life's unexpected expenses, such as car repair?

☞ Do you know if you are saving enough for retirement?

☞ Do you know where your retirement money is, and what it is invested in?

If you answered no to more than a couple of these, you are probably living in a money fog.

When one is in the money fog, one is uncertain where one is, where one has been, or where one is going, financially. Many women live under this vague but persistent sense of anxiety and foreboding. Some describe it as "always waiting for the other shoe to drop." Others describe it as a chronic worry about money— one that never leaves entirely, but may fade to the back for a while, only to jump front and center at the next financial crisis.

Many women assume that if they only earned more, their money problems would go away. But as long as one is living in a financial fog, one can not and will not earn more money. Earning more money does not vanquish the fog. However, eliminating the money fog can have a direct impact on your ability to earn more money. When we are in a money fog, we are usually in denial about what we are doing with our money, and this denial makes it difficult to change. Karen McCall says it well in her *MoneyMinder Financial Recovery Workbook* (Financial Recovery Press, 2002), "If you are vague about your money situation or habits, or if you feel that you have no control over your money, it's very difficult to connect your money behaviors with their consequences. And it is virtually impossible to take concrete steps towards change."

Women who are not underearners are more likely to know where their money goes, how much they are making, and how much they owe in debt. They tend to carry very little debt in the first place, and are usually good savers. Underearners, on the other hand, usually have no clue where their money is going, and hence usually have credit card debt. They rarely balance their checkbooks and usually don't contribute to a retirement plan. In addition, they tend to obsess over money, worrying how everything will work out. They are used to living from paycheck to paycheck, and from financial crisis to financial crisis. Of course no one has all of these characteristics, but any one of them can lead one down a perilous financial road. When a woman is financially vague, it can spell nothing less than disaster.

When We Enable Ourselves

Let me introduce you to the golden rule of underearning: *Never take a job that pays less than is enough for you.* I realize this sounds simple, and I know it is not. But if you never take a job that pays less than is enough, you will never underearn. The core problem is that many women do not know how much they need. And if you don't know exactly how much enough is, how can you avoid underearning? (I will discuss the definition of "enough" in Chapter 6.)

There are two specific behaviors people engage in that enable them to continue underearning. They are

1. Incurring debt (in all its forms).

2. Poor record keeping.

These behaviors are not the cause of underearning. Rather, these behaviors allow women to continue underearning, without being aware they are doing so. These behaviors make it almost impossible to stop underearning. Therefore, it is extremely important to examine them.

Think of it this way. There are some financial behaviors that many people routinely fall into that actually hide their underearning. As you will see, for example, when you carry a lot of debt, it can be hard to see that you may not be making enough money. These financial behaviors, all rooted in vagueness, can actually help keep you in denial. All your focus might be consumed by your debt or having to juggle finances. You may be in constant crisis management, juggling credit cards and trying to figure out just how much money you actually have. But these behaviors may be diverting you from the source of your problems: perhaps you are not making enough money in the first place.

When I give seminars on underearning, and I ask participants afterwards what they found the most valuable, often they will tell me, "It was the enabling part. I never realized how I was actually helping myself underearn!" So read on and see if you are also helping yourself to underearn.

Debt

Many people know that credit card debt is a major problem for millions of people in the United States, though most do not realize how far the problem extends. As of 2002, according to *Cardweb.com*, 59 percent of Americans carried a credit card balance, meaning they do not pay their balances off in full each month. And the average credit card debt per household? For households with at least one credit card, the average debt is $8,562. This is spread over eight credit cards, which is the average number of cards per cardholder. (Households on average hold 14 different charge cards, including bank cards and retail store cards. This does not include debit cards.) And an estimated 20 percent of credit cards are maxed out!

One of the problems with credit cards is the interest that accrues on unpaid balances. Many Americans dutifully pay on their credit card debt each month, but for those 59 percent carrying a balance, they are not making much progress. Let's look at a single example that illustrates the problem with paying minimum payments, which so many people do. If you owe $3,000 on a credit card at 18-percent interest, and you pay the minimum payments (usually about 2 percent of the balance) until it is paid off, it will take you 451 months to pay off. That is more than 37 years! And all of this assumes you never add any new debt to the credit card. It's pretty startling (and depressing) when you really look at the numbers.

But the impact of debt is much farther reaching than people suspect. *Debt creates the illusion that there is enough money.* Using credit cards can blind us to the fact that we are not earning enough. Think about it this way. In a simple world, many people would live within their means for a certain portion of the month. Then, towards the end of the month, they would begin to run out of cash. At this point, many people would simply whip out their credit cards to continue spending. They may feel it is the only way to make it through the month. Credit cards pick up where their earnings fall short.

Of course in the real world, it is more complex. Most people don't spend cash until they run out, and then pull out plastic. People use credit cards here and there, throughout the month, sometimes not thinking that they are using the card because they do not have enough money. (I also know many people who use cards for their airline miles. The question is if the negative affect of using a credit card outweighs their accumulated miles....But that is a debate for another time.) The truth is that when you use credit cards, it makes it very hard to both see how much you are spending, and hence, how much you need to be making.

When you have access to debt, regardless of whether it is a personal loan, your overdraft checking, or a credit card, you do not have to live in the pain of feeling there is not enough money. When you experience financial stress, you may simply whip out your "emergency backup," as so many have been taught to think about credit cards. Instead of being forced to find a way to come up with more money, you bail yourself out.

You may be thinking there really are legitimate times to use credit cards. Perhaps. But once again, step into a simple world for a moment. Imagine a world with no debt. You are debt free. Furthermore, you can't have debt. You do not have the ability to borrow money. No matter what, in this world, you can't borrow from a friend or pull out a credit card. You can't borrow money, period. (Remember, using a credit card is a potent form of borrowing—you are simply "borrowing" money from a lender, and promising to pay it back at a future date, with interest.)

Now, what would happen in this world if you realized you didn't have enough money? What would you do if you realized you were not making enough money to pay your bills? First, you would feel scared. That is true. You would have to live in the pain of knowing that you are not making enough money. And then, most likely, you would use your creative powers to come up with a way to make more. You would have the incentive to make sure you were paid appropriately, and you would seek jobs that paid you enough money—because you would have to. But in our world, people have been robbed of this incentive. In our world, not only can you just use a credit card when it gets tough, you can use debt so much that you don't even know if you are making enough money or not. Debt keeps people vague. But as Jerrold Mundis puts it so clearly, in *Earn What You Deserve* (Bantam Books, 1995), "The very act of borrowing, of using credit, of not paying a bill on time, is a clear signal that you are gaining less income then you need. And so long as you consider the use of some form of debt to be a valid option for meeting your needs, then it is nearly impossible that you will become free of underearning."

Credit cards rob you of your creativity, and they rob you of your incentive. When you can fall back on using a card, you do not have to think of a more creative way to meet your needs or wants. So, if you want to stop underearning, one of the first things you must do is stop debting.

Credit cards are also about giving your energy away. This may sound metaphysical, but think of it this way. When you owe money, it is as if a piece of you is owned by different creditors. Part of financial recovery is pulling back these pieces of yourself.

Credit cards also keep you in the status quo, and limit your potential for growth. When you are in debt, it has the effect of keeping you from moving forward. When you owe a lot of money, you can't take advantage of different opportunities that may come your way.

LaDonna felt dissatisfied with her job. She longed to try something new. At one point, a wonderful opportunity came along. A new start-up company, which was creating an exciting new product and service for consumers, approached her and asked if she wanted to join them. She could have gotten in on the ground floor, which meant low initial pay, but also a possibly huge payoff down the road. LaDonna debated about this opportunity for days. It was an exciting chance to leave the job she'd grown tired of. And she believed in what this new company was trying to create. But LaDonna was maxed out on all her cards and up to her eyeballs in consumer debt. She literally couldn't afford to make less money—in many ways, she was imprisoned in her current position.

Some of you may be confused. Wouldn't LaDonna be underearning if she took a lower paying job? Not necessarily. Remember, underearning is not about earning a specific dollar figure. It is about earning enough money for you. If LaDonna carried less debt, she could have taken a lower paying job that she enjoyed more and still have had her needs met. But debt cut off her options and required her to make a certain amount of money in order to service her debt.

Ask yourself, has debt ever kept you from seizing an opportunity?

A Wider Definition of Debt

I want to give you a wider definition of debt than I suspect you are used to. I would define debt as borrowing money from someone else, *or* borrowing money from yourself. So for example, if you are "borrowing" money from your 401(k), I would consider that a debt. (This is not the place to discuss the pros and cons of tapping your 401(k) to buy a house.) In addition, whenever someone dips into one of their long-term investments, because they need money in the present, I would consider that a debt. For example, you run short of money, so you have to raid that old IRA account, or you have to sell some stock, or part of a mutual fund. I would consider it "debting" if you are using the money for something other than for what it was intended, which was usually long-term investment objectives.

The problem with borrowing money in this way is similar to using a credit card. When you "borrow" from your investments, you do not have to face up to the truth that you are not making enough money. Using long-term money in this way allows people to continue underearning, without having to face the problem. And it is perhaps all the more insidious because it is your money. Because many people don't see raiding investments as a form of debting, this can go unchecked. You never have the same incentive to either get a job or make enough money, because you always have this pot of money to raid.

During one class on underearning that I taught, this point, in particular, really hit home. There were several women in the class who did not see themselves as struggling a great deal financially, but sensed that they were underearning, and wanted to make more money. But these women also confessed to consistently drawing money from their investments in order to get by. They also talked about how stressful it was for them to watch their savings dwindle, but felt that they had no choice.

"I've been living off my investments for the past six months, as I keep trying to find a new job. I realize now that I haven't had the same incentive to find new work because I have this pile of money to draw from. Otherwise, I suspect I would already have found my next job. And this money was supposed to be for my future."

The Curse of Inherited Wealth

Inheriting wealth can be a curse. Of course most people would vehemently argue the opposite, but inherited wealth can be very detrimental to one's sense of self-reliance. When a woman grows up in a wealthy family, and has access to family money as an adult, she has very little incentive to try to make it on her own in the world. Many inheritors long to have their own career, but they are notorious underearners—earning far below their capacity—because their wealth inhibits their drive. While their friends with less money may envy them, chances are that they envy those friends for their success in the work-place. When people do not grow up with a lot of money, they are forced to learn to support themselves, and when they do they gain heart-felt knowledge that they can take care of them-selves. Many inheritors don't have this deep-felt knowledge. This knowledge is very important to one's self-esteem, and abil-ity to be fully independent. Many inheritors wander through life from job to job, never able to build a meaningful career, despite a genuine desire to do so, and as a result, their self-esteem suffers.

Imagine growing up with money and knowing you will nev-er have to support yourself. You will always be taken care of. This may sound wonderful to people who do not have a lot of money, but the fact is that many inheritors have a very diffi-cult time reaching their full potential. Often times, they never really know how far they could have taken something, because their inheritance robbed them of the financial incentive to push a project through, or reach a certain goal. Money can be a wonderful motivator. Without this motivation, it can be diffi-cult to see just how far your abilities can take you.

But sometimes the problem is not as immediately visible, because the sums of money involved are much smaller. Although most people do not grow up with inherited wealth, it is very com-mon to inherit at least a small portion of money at some point in one's life. And these smaller portions can act as "bail-outs," curtailing our ability to see something through on our own.

Teresa and her husband worked hard to build their careers during the first few years of their marriage. It was not always easy. Teresa's therapy practice was fledgling, and with a habit of not marketing herself properly, she struggled to build her client base. They were forced to occasionally use credit cards to make ends meet, although they promised themselves this would only be a temporary situation. But the debt mounted. Then, Teresa's uncle died, and left them $40,000. They put this money in a savings account, intending to use it for retirement and their children's college education. But they kept dipping into the account for living expenses, and used part of it to pay off some of their debt. Eventually, after five years, they had spent all the money that they had inherited. Still they struggled with their careers. Two years after the money ran out, her husband inherited $10,000 dollars from one of his relatives. Again, they intended to invest the money, but again, they used it for day-to-day living expenses.

Teresa was never forced to really assess her career and her business decisions. She continued to marginally market her practice, and to obtain marginal results. But whenever things seemed really bad, money magically fell into their laps. This "magic" money had the effect of never forcing them to get serious about their earning problems. In effect, they drew from a constantly dwindling pile of money, forever uncertain as to what they needed to live, and what they needed to make. These sporadic windfalls made it so they were never forced to take a hard look at their finances and admit that they did not make enough. The money, in effect, kept them from ever working to their full potential.

A Word to Parents

It is a particularly sensitive issue when I talk with parents about giving their grown children money. Remember Eleanor, and her guilt over her daughter Michelle? She felt her daughter's lack of financial success as an adult reflected on her parenting. Ideally, we instill in our children a respect for money, and a healthy work ethic. But when grown children stumble, some parents immediately give them money to fix the problem. And when we constantly bail out our adult children, we are in effect enabling them to continue not supporting themselves.

I often ask parents, "What would happen if you did not give Suzy any money this time?" They answer that she would be out on the streets, or that something else equally horrible would happen. Usually, this is overly dramatic. Suzy would most likely learn to support herself. But if Suzy had been taught good financial habits from the start, and always knew that it would be up to her to support herself as an adult, it might have gone differently. I've met with many parents who are supporting their 19- and 20-year-old children, some of whom are not working, and some of whom are only working part time. (I'm not talking about children living with parents while they are going to college. This can be a wonderful way to support your children in their college aspirations, particularly if you can't put actual money towards tuition.) What would happen if these children were not given money? They would have to rely on themselves and find work. Giving money to children can enable them in their underearning.

Are there sometimes when it is appropriate to give money to our adult children? Of course there are. We want the best for them, and many of us want to be generous with the money we do have. But we need to ask ourselves the effect this money has on them. Sometimes, it is truly needed and appreciated. Other times, it simply reinforces the message that they will constantly be bailed out. When parents consistently bail out their adult children, children have a way of taking their parents, and their money, for granted. As with so many issues surrounding money, the important thing is to be *conscious* in our decision to give money to our children—not to do it out of sheer habit, or guilt.

I would also add that it is particularly dangerous to raid one's investments for one's children. I've known many parents who cashed in part of their retirement savings for their children, sometimes for something as noble as college funding. But remember that children can borrow money for college, but you can not borrow money to retire. This is a crucial difference.

Poor Record Keeping

"I just need to make more money!" was LaDonna's frequent answer to the questions I posed to her. Maybe, but when I asked her how much she needed to be earning, she could not give me a dollar amount.

It is very frustrating to feel like you are not making enough money. Many people feel this way, but if you don't know how much you need to live, how can you figure out exactly how much you would need to earn?

The cure for vagueness is careful record keeping, and record keeping is comprised of two tasks: tracking where your money goes, and managing your checking accounts. How many of you are suddenly ready to shut this book? Where is the talk about underearning? Hang in there—you'll see the connection.

The very first thing I had LaDonna start doing was to track where her money was going. She experienced tremendous resistance to this. Part of it was that she felt she didn't have the time to write down everything she spent. And she admitted that another part of her did not want to see where all her money was going. I assured her that this was a necessary step to her financial recovery. I gave her a blank spending plan and showed her how to record her spending at the end of every day.

Another part of her resistance was the perception that only people who have problems with money need to track their finances in this way. This is a common belief, and yet the truth is the exact opposite. Women who earn a lot of money are far more likely to know where their money goes than women who

are underearning. The women who earn more know that tracking their spending is a useful tool to building and keeping
wealth—not a sign of poverty.

I was in graduate school when I was first introduced to
these concepts by Karen McCall of the Financial Recovery
Institute. My husband and I had very little money, and we
coped with it by spending as little money as humanly possible.
When I started on my own financial recovery, I started by
tracking where our money was really going. I carried around
a small green spiral notebook, where I made notes about
everything that I spent. It was difficult at first, and awkward.
I felt like I was always fumbling for that spiral notebook. At
night, I would transfer the numbers to a spending plan, where
I could track the big picture of what was happening. And I
was shocked when I saw how things added up. My latte habit
alone was more than $50 a month!

As it so often is, this rude awakening was painful. But within
a few months, we began to experience a new sense of peace
concerning money. We stopped using the credit card, and
began to work on paying the balance down. We started to plan
where we wanted our money to go. And instead of living in fear
that there was not enough, we gained clarity about what was
happening and what was possible. I began to feel more in control,
because I could now clearly see where I was going and what I
was doing. I also started to see how much I actually needed to
be making. This was the beginning of my true career planning.
I decided what I wanted to be earning, and then began to plan
accordingly in with my career. What a difference! Instead of
life just happening, I was plotting a course towards a better
life where we were free from financial stress and life was full of
possibility!

I also had LaDonna start using her checkbook register again.
In fact, I had to give her a new register, since it had been years
since she had used one. Usually, she only had a general sense
of how much was in her account. If she needed a balance, she

called the bank. And she thought that method was fine, because she bounced checks "only" a couple of times a year.

I call this form of checking playing the game of "virtual checking." It is amazing the amount of energy people expend trying to track their finances in their heads. When one actually writes things down in a register or on the computer, it is as if it actually frees up mental capacity, for use on something else. In LaDonna's case, I simply had her start recording any transactions that would affect her account balance, such as checks and debit transactions. After a few weeks, we undertook balancing her account. Eventually, she came to like knowing exactly where she was and how much she had—much more than just trying to keep track of things in her head. She said that it gave her a peace of mind that allowed her to focus on other things.

It is well worth your time to start keeping better track of your money. When you are conscious of where your money is going, you become more grounded in the reality of your life. If you don't like the reality you see, then this disconnect can be a great impetus to change. Again, Karen McCall writes in the *MoneyMinder Financial Recovery Workbook* (Financial Recovery Press, 2002), "Being disconnected from our money is a way of being disconnected from ourselves. It is what causes us to act against our own best interest. To realize the financial life you want to live, you need to find a way to become conscious of what you are doing with money." When you are conscious, you can purposely create the life you want.

If you are not currently keeping a checkbook register, whether it be a manual (paper) register, or computer register (such as Quicken), make it a point to begin doing so. I've discovered that many adults simply do not know how to balance a checking account. They either were never taught, or their partners kept the books. Sometimes, it has been so many years since they paid that close attention to their finances, they simply don't remember and are out of the habit. The simplest way to begin is to just carry a checkbook register around with you and begin recording in it any time you access your account. For most people, this means they need to write down the checks they write, as well as their debit transactions, and they need to write in all the automatic transactions so many people have. (Here's a tip: If you have a hard time writing down all your debits in your check book register, clip your debit card inside your register. That way any time you need your debit card, you will have to open your register!) If you do not know how to balance your account, ask a trusted friend who you know balances theirs. Though it can be hard to ask, most friends would be more then happy to share their knowledge with you. And they will be flattered that you asked them.

The absolute most effective way to truly keep track of your finances, beside staying in control of your checking account and knowing at any given moment how much you have in the bank, is to create and keep a spending plan. Similar to a budget, a spending plan is your monthly plan for how you would like to spend your money. You create a spending plan, and then track on it where your money actually goes. At the end of the month, it is an effective tool for analyzing what is actually happening in your life and can show you how you can better reach your goals. If you would like to learn how to work with a spending plan, contact the Financial Recovery Institute (*www.financialrecovery.com*) and order their Complete MoneyMinder System. It is one of the best tools out there to guide people through the process of creating and keeping a realistic spending plan.

Why We Stay in the Fog...

Obviously, living in a financial fog is detrimental to our lives, so why do so many women live this way? One reason is rooted in the Romance Myth—women are sometimes adverse to being fiscally responsible. They insist on not taking control of their finances because they persist in their belief that it is not all up to them—that sooner or later, Prince Charming will ride in and lift them out of the fog into a better life—the life they always envisioned they would lead.

Some of you may be saying, "But it really isn't my fault that I am on the edge, financially. The deck is stacked against me." And you may be correct. There is no denying that gender discrimination in the workplace is alive and well. But gender discrimination accounts for only a part of the wage discrepancy between men and women. Remember, overcoming underearning requires acknowledging the part you personally play in earning money. And the truth is that many women are out of control with the money they do have. While the amount of money women make varies greatly, underearners live as if it were not all up to them to take control of their financial lives. They resist taking responsibility by refusing to manage their checkbooks, or they insist on staying vague as to where their money goes. This vagueness cannot be blamed on gender discrimination and glass ceilings.

Some women stay in the money fog because they honestly don't know that they are in one. If you've been in a fog your whole life, it is all that you know. It is like growing up in a polluted city. Then one day you hike up a mountain outside the city and see the smog smothering the populace. Sometimes, it is not until you are out of a fog that you can see the depth of the fog you managed to pull out of. I find this usually to be the case. As I help clients clear away a layer of financial vagueness, we often find yet another layer of fog, a level they weren't even aware of.

Some women may realize dimly that they are in a fog, but simply don't possess the skills to climb out. And still others continue on in the fog because they are unaware of the true impact the fog is having on them. I believe many women fall in this last category. Women may know they're foggy, or somewhat out of control with their money, but they rarely realize the dire consequences of this. Think of it this way: If one drives around in

the fog long enough, it is not a matter of *if* you will hit something, it is a matter of *when* you will hit something. How big an
accident will you have? Perhaps only a bounced check,
perhaps bankruptcy. But the affect the fog has on your long
term earning ability is the biggest accident of all. Unfortunately, it is this accident that so many women don't foresee.

The Money-life Drain

The point of conquering underearning is not to work as
much as possible. The point is to be conscious about your earning,
and to know what you need. Perhaps, the clearer you are, the
less you will need, and the less you will have to work. For
example, if you decide to bring your expenses down, then you
won't need to bring home as much money.

When women are unconscious, and hence, vague, they may
have to work more than they really need to, in an effort to "keep
up" their spending. Karen McCall, founder of the Financial
Recovery Institute, talks about the "money-life drain," which
shows the downward spiral that happens as out-of-control
expenses force you to work more and have less time. She says
that at first, people try to shoulder their financial burdens, which
are usually comprised of debt and out-of-control expenses. This
debt and out-of-control spending means you have to make more
money, in order to pay your debt and have money to maintain
your lifestyle. Hence, you have an increased pressure to earn,
coupled with the inability to save, because your money is
already spoken for. From here, relationships often become
stressed. In McCall's book, *It's Your Money: Achieving Financial
Well-Being* (Chronical Books, 2000), she writes "When you
are unable to save and are pressured to work more and earn
more, your relationships become strained, your health is
impacted by stress, and ultimately your overall quality of life
deteriorates."

The money-life drain illustrates what happens when women live inside a money fog. Many people are caught in this drain. They are tired of having to work constantly, and battling to always get ahead, which they never seem able to do. Clearly, the answer is not to merely work more. Often, when people do work more, they are so stressed out that they also spend more. They take expensive vacations, and buy expensive clothes. "Hey, I work hard. I deserve to take a vacation!" is the common refrain. And the money-life drain just continues, slowly draining you. But if you are conscious about your money, then perhaps you will see that you do not have to work as hard or as much. Remember, the point is not to make as much money as humanly possible, but to be conscious of your earnings and to know how much "enough" really is.

Ask yourself, is money worthy of your time? If it is, then it deserves to have time and attention devoted to it. If you become clearer about your finances, you stand a much better chance of knowing how much you need to be making. And it makes it difficult to live in a financial fog, a fog where you may be underearning and not even know it.

People who underearn and live in a financial fog often have chronic, low-level stress, because they know, if only unconsciously, that their lives are out of control. The good news is that the road to peace of mind is a simple one. It involves something that I call "radical clarity"—meaning that a person knows from where every cent is coming , and were it is going to. I ask all of my clients to practice "radical clarity," and you may want to practice it too. It is through use of this practice that you will blow away the money fog, and become more conscious about your finances. It will help you live a life that has less stress, and more peace of mind. When you know where your resources are going, you can't help but become more conscious!

Before you dismiss the idea of radical clarity, ask yourself, are your current habits around money helping you or hindering you? You are in control of your money. It works for you, not you for it. Are you living to work, or working to live? Ideally, you are working so you can lead a more fulfilling life.

There is no question that the money fog facilitates under-earning. Being in the money fog means you are unclear as to how much you need to be making, because you are unclear about how much you are spending. So, if you want to earn more money, stop enabling yourself to underearn. If you don't have enough money, it is time to face up to this painful truth, and do something about it. Stop hiding in the fog.

The effects of underearning follow us throughout our life, depriving us of truly enjoying life in the present and hitting us the hardest in the future. It is far better to face the truth now, however painful that truth may be, and to begin to plot a course towards a better life.

Now that you are clear about how you are enabling your-self to continue underearning, through vagueness and debt, you can begin to see what you need. It is time to decide exactly how much you need to earn, to live the life that you want.

Chapter Six

How Much Is Enough?

"If only I made more money, I wouldn't have these financial problems!"

Teresa was in my office, complaining about not making enough money.

"How much more money, exactly, would you need to be making?" I asked.

"Well, I'm not sure. More than I do now, anyway!"

"And how much do you make right now?" I queried.

There was a long pause, while Teresa added numbers in her head.

"Well, I'm not really sure about that either, to tell you the truth. There's the money from my private practice, and then there is the outpatient treatment program work I do, part time. And of course when I run a lot of therapy groups, more money comes in."

Teresa and I went on to talk about how she set up her private practice. I asked her how much she was charging.

"Eighty dollars an hour."

I privately wondered if she was really making that much. In fact, I suspected that Teresa was living in a money fog, unsure of both how much she actually earned, and how much she needed to make. So I gave her some homework. I told her to list every single one of her clients and then, next to their name, write down how much they actually paid her. When she did this, the list showed that some clients were on a sliding scale, a few she bartered with, and many paid her through insurance claims that paid out different amounts of money. Only a few actually paid her the standard $80 an hour. We added up all the different hourly fees, and divided by her total number of clients. It came out to $52.40 an hour.

"I can't believe I'm only making 52 bucks an hour! And then you take out expenses and taxes....No wonder I'm not getting ahead!"

Again, I posed the question: "Exactly how much more do you think you need to be making?" But she couldn't say. And without a clear picture, she wasn't able to make a game plan.

Teresa had a classic underearning problem—lack of clarity. If you don't know how much you need to be making, how can you avoid underearning? Teresa just figured that because the clinic where she now worked paid better than what she had been doing previously, she should take the job. The problem is that even if a job pays more than a previous job, if it still pays less than you need, you will still be underearning. And without knowing how much you need, it is hard to target the right job and ask for an appropriate amount of money.

I've encountered many people who feel that they are not making enough money. They seem to think that if they only made more, their problems would automatically go away. Have you ever said, *If only I made more money?* Well, exactly how much more would be enough? I've found that most people don't know precisely what "enough" means to them.

How Much Is "Enough?"

Often, when people talk about making enough money, they have a specific dollar figure in mind. "If only I made $60,000, then I could pay off my debt." "If only I made more than $18 an hour, I could start saving for that house down payment." But in reality, if you ask them where they got these figures, they probably couldn't tell you. The numbers just sound good—that is, they are more than what they are currently making.

Yes, it is important to come up with a specific number—the amount you would need to earn to avoid underearning. And that is what this chapter is about. But before you can talk about specific numbers, it is important to discuss what one means by the term "enough."

I use a special definition of "enough" in my work, and it's a very important one. A person is making "enough" money, by definition, if there is money to cover three things:

1. Basic needs.

2. Wants/desires.

3. Savings.

If you are not earning enough money to cover all three of these, then you are underearning. Let's look at these more closely.

First of all, women need to make enough money to cover their needs. This is the easiest part of the definition. You need to make enough to cover your food, shelter, clothing, and other basic necessities. However, even though this part of the definition is easy to understand, it does not mean that everyone has this covered. I know many people who spend money on many of their "wants," but do not have health insurance, or other things I would categorize as a "need."

Second, women need to make enough to cover their wants. This is the most subjective part of the definition. Different people see wants differently. What is a want to one person is a need to another, and vice versa. I like to define this part of the definition as "enough money to enjoy life." As I tell my clients, the point is not to spend as little as humanly possible. After all, knowing that this is the only life we get, it is only fair that we should enjoy some of it! Underearners tend to not spend enough money in this category. Women who have lived a life of underearning tend to also have lived a life of deprivation. In fact, many women actually feel guilty when they spend money on themselves. This is a mistake. You have to feel that you are worth having money spent on you!

Figuring out a woman's wants requires her to be clear about how she wants to live her life, and what she values. I value leisure time. So, for example, part of my "wants" is having the time and money to pursue my own hobbies. And my husband and I love science fiction, so we know that when a great science fiction movie comes out, we are going to spend the money on a babysitter, movie tickets, and popcorn. Other movies can wait for video. We know what makes us happy. What makes you happy? How would you choose to spend money to enjoy life more?

The third part of the definition is about savings. Women need to make enough to cover their savings. This is usually the part that gets left out. By savings, I mean enough money to save for large purchases and trips, so that we don't have to wrack up credit card debt. This is also about being prepared for the unexpected. And, it is about enough money to save for the future. That's right, retirement. *If you are not making enough money to save for your retirement, you are underearning.* (There is one exception here: Inheritors may not need to be saving for retirement. However, they may still be underearners because they are working below their potential.)

This is where underearning can feel very insidious. Many women cover their needs, and even some of their wants, right now. It's hard to ignore the present. But when you don't save for retirement, you don't feel the effects of this lack of money until the future. The future is where underearning impacts you the most. And according to the National Center for Women and Retirement Research, nearly 70 percent of women say they have no idea how much they'll need for retirement. A lifetime of having your wants and needs covered will pale in meaning when you become older and there is suddenly no money to cover them anymore. This is the plight of countless women. It is what spawns nightmares of the Bag Lady.

Some people would add a fourth part of the definition. You are making "enough" money when you can cover needs, wants, savings, and charitable/philanthropic giving. Because this is a very personal choice, I will not include it in the general definition, but many people feel strongly about having enough money to give back to the world. (However, I don't believe you should emphasize the fourth part until the first three are in place. Otherwise, if you are giving money away and you don't have enough for yourself, you will jeopardize your ability to give money away in the future.)

Now we can go back to the "Golden Rule" of underearning. To avoid underearning, *never take a job that pays less than is enough for you.* Let this definition guide you in your journey to overcome underearning.

✎ Exercise: Your Earning Ceiling ✐

Before you begin to think of specific numbers, I want you to spend some time meditating on your "earning ceiling." By that, I mean the salary above which you can't imagine earning. Almost everyone has an internal earning ceiling. It is important to be aware of it, because otherwise, it will be almost impossible to rise above it. Write the following numbers down on a piece of paper, going down the left hand side. Leave plenty of space to write after the numbers.

$15,000	$100,000
$25,000	$250,000
$50,000	$500,000
$75,000	$1,000,000

Now, get comfortable, and start thinking about the first number. Ask yourself these questions: How does it feel to be making $15,000? What does my life look like? What am I doing? What am I not doing? Who is there? How does it really feel to be making $15,000?

Meditate thoroughly on each number, using these questions, before going on to the next. Then, when you are done, go to your piece of paper and write down any thoughts, feelings, or images that came to you for each number.

This exercise was developed by Karen McCall, the founder of the Financial Recovery Institute. She says that when she is in a large room of people doing this exercise, she can tell where people start to hit their earning ceilings. When she mentions a certain number, some people start to squirm, look uncomfortable, or start to giggle. I've found the same thing when I use this in groups.

I remember very clearly the first time I did this meditation. When I hit the $50,000 mark, it was as if I hit a blank wall. I just couldn't go any farther. When I really meditated on it, all I could see was my father sitting on this wall. What was he doing there? Then I realized he was actually busy working, but blocking my way nonetheless. As I continued to meditate on this, it came to me that $50,000 was the most my father ever earned (or so I thought at the time), and I just couldn't imagine earning more than him. If the most my father ever earned was $50,000, who was I to surpass him? To do so felt a betrayal to him, for all the hard years of work he put in. I had somehow picked up the message that it wasn't okay to surpass my parents.

And I feared that my parents, who had always unconditionally supported me, might withdraw some of their support if I made more money than they did. Their support has been one of the most important things in my life, and the thought of losing it, as irrational as it seemed, stopped me in my tracks. My underearning therefore served to keep me in line with what I thought my family believed I should be making. It served to keep me from surpassing my father and ensured they would continue to lend me their emotional support. It was only when I could clearly see what my income ceiling was, and why, that I was able to break through it.

continually have to contend with our internal limitations. Until we reach that space of limitless possibility, we will carry around within us various barriers and ceilings. Just know that they are not permanent. When we bump up against them, it is just a sign that we are pushing some internal buttons about what we think we are truly capable of, and we must do the internal work until we believe we really are worth this next level of money.

Fearing Our Number

When people begin to think about how much money would be enough for them, strong feelings often arise. At first, many people fear that if they really knew how much they needed to be making, they would discover that this amount was beyond their abilities. *I'll never be able to make that much money! Now what do I do?* It almost seems like it is better to not know. And that is what many women do—choose not to know. They fear that if they saw what they really needed to be making, they would be overwhelmed by the changes that would be required of them. Would they have to get a better job? Would they have to ask for a raise, or go back to school? These are scary propositions, and many women would prefer not to face them. After all, they require that you leave your comfort zone, and it is change that we fear the most.

I talked with Financial Recovery Counselor/Coach Denise Hughes about this. "Underearners are scared to death to see what they really need to be making. If they see the amount, they worry they will be overwhelmed and depressed by it. But I always tell them, 'There is no freedom in ignorance.'"

And she is right. Knowledge is power. If you know what you need to be earning, then you stand a much better chance of earning that amount. To remain ignorant of your needed earnings is to remain a slave to a present work situation that may no longer be serving you.

There is another possible reaction to seeing the amount one needs to earn in order to make enough. Sometimes, people

When Judy, our events planner, did this meditation, she could visualize the lower numbers pretty well. At $15,000, she saw trailer parks. At $50,000, she saw a modest but nice house in the suburbs. But when she hit $100,000, she noticed a strange thing. There were no people in her meditation. At that amount and more, she was alone.

When Judy reflected on this, she realized it was the Romance Myth at work once again. If she made more than $100,000, why would anyone come and take care of her? Who would swoop down to rescue her? Surely she would be on her own—self-sufficient, but lonely. She also realized that somewhere in the mix was the persistent notion that many people do not like the wealthy. She herself had mixed feelings about them. If she made a lot of money, would her friends still like her?

Once Judy became aware of these feelings, she was able to think about them, feel them, and process them. When they remained unconscious, she was taking action (or doing nothing) based on unconscious fears of what would happen. Once she was aware of how a part of her felt, she was able to talk about it, journal about these feelings, and begin to give herself new beliefs through the use of affirmations. For example, she would practice saying to herself, "I am worthy of being loved, regardless of how much money I make."

So where did you get stopped? At what point was it hazy? At what amount did it become difficult to see what your life looked like? If you made more than this earning ceiling, what are you afraid would happen, or stop happening? Would you lose something if you made more than this, or would you be forced to do something you don't want to do?

Keep in mind that glass ceilings are not static. Our ceiling will continue to change as we change. We may find ourselves bumping up against our ceiling for a time, and then eventually break through it. But at some point, we run into another ceiling. Our ceiling doesn't usually disappear, it just moves higher. As we develop and make more money throughout our lives, we will are shocked to see that the amount isn't that much greater than what they are currently making. Then they are faced with the liberating fact that it is possible to live a wider, more expansive life without changing too much. This is what clarity can do.

Finally, we must recognize that sometimes it's not the actual numbers that are a problem, but our inability to imagine a better life for ourselves. When you have lived a restricted life for many years, it can be challenging to envision living differently. But doing so is a vital step to overcoming underearning.

Creating an "Earnings Plan"

You are about to create an earnings plan. Simply put, you are going to decide how much money you want and need to make, based on how much money you want to spend. You will take into account all parts of the "enough" definition I discussed previously: needs, wants, and savings, and you will also learn how to differentiate between what you need to "gross" versus what you need to "net" (meaning, what you have before taxes, and what you have afterwards). But before we go into all of this, consider what approach you will take with this exercise.

You could do this exercise from a "barebones" perspective. This means that you would determine what is the least amount of money you could spend in each category. Sometimes, this is helpful in seeing what your true bottom line is. What is the least amount of money you could earn and still be okay? However, underearners already tend to not spend enough, and to think in terms of absolute needs, as opposed to how much it would take to make life truly enjoyable. When one has dealt with a lot of deprivation in one's life, it is best not to approach this exercise with a "What is the least I can spend?" mentality. (Not doing so may be a challenge for those of you wrestling with noble poverty.) Can you allow your vision of your life to expand?

On the other hand, you could approach this exercise with the thought, "What would my ideal life look like?" But again, this can be difficult for underearners. When it is hard to spend

money on oneself, it is hard to think about one's "ideal" life.
And also, when one looks only at the ideal, the numbers can
feel scary. True, your ideal life might be lived on the French
Rivera, but the numbers involved would be overwhelming.

So how do you start? The answer is somewhere between
these two extremes. Imagine a comfortable life where there is
enough money. I would suggest you read the following passage
and then close the book and meditate on it. I would also recommend you spend some time journaling about this, before you
move on to creating your actual earnings plan.

> In a nice, quiet place, spend some time relaxing your
> body and getting comfortable. Do whatever you need
> to do to feel fully present within yourself. Then, begin
> to imagine a life where there is "enough." Your needs
> are covered, you are enjoying doing the things you like,
> and you are saving for your future. How does this feel?
> What do you see? Who is there? Where are you? Spend
> time imagining what your life would feel like if there
> were enough money. You are not financially stressed
> and you know in your heart that there is enough money
> to do the things you need to do and enjoy doing in life.
> Rest in this vision and let it permeate your body. This
> is what "enough" feels like. Now you can begin creat-
> ing your earnings plan.

The Numbers

Creating an earnings plan is similar to creating a spending
plan. As Financial Recovery Counselors, we work with clients to
create personalized spending plans. When one creates a spending plan, one is deciding how much one wants to spend in each
category for a given month. Then one tracks their actual spending during the month, and at the end of the month, the plan is
compared to what actually happened. It is beyond the scope
and purpose of this book to teach people how to maintain a

spending plan process. (Though maintaining a spending plan process is one of the most powerful and useful things you can do. If you are interested in learning how to plan your spending, consider contacting the Financial Recovery Institute to either buy their Complete MoneyMinder System, or to find a financial counselor to work with.) However, you will be using categories from an actual spending plan to create your earnings plan.

There are three steps to creating an earnings plan. It is not enough to simply go through spending categories for the month and decide what you need, and then multiply that number by 12 months. If you do that, the amount you come up with will be far below the amount of money you actually need to live. This is because you have numerous periodic expenses during the year—expenses that don't come up every month. For example, you might learn that you need unexpected dental work. Or perhaps you will have a fender bender. So first, you need to determine how much you need for periodic expenses, those things that seem to always "pop up," and then you need to go back and think about an average month. Lastly we will deal with taxes.

So it's time to grab a pencil and start filling in some numbers. This exercise usually takes a couple of days. Take all the time you need to really think about how much "enough" would be for you. Some people get a notebook and write down these categories, personalizing them for themselves as they go. Some people also go back through their checkbook registers to try to obtain more realistic numbers. It is up to you. Obviously, the more data you have, the easier it will be to come up with realistic numbers, but don't let not having data stop you from doing this exercise. Any idea as to what you need to earn is better than none at all. Simply do the best you can.

Step One: Calculate Your Annual Periodics

As mentioned previously, periodics are expenses that pop up on an irregular basis. They tend to be what cause people so much trouble, especially when they haven't anticipated them and put money aside for them. For example, you may feel that you are making enough money, but when August rolls around and it's time for your annual vacation at the beach, you don't have enough to cover the hotel bill. Or you never save for Christmas, so you end up paying for gifts with credit cards. These are periodics—all part of the ebb and flow of our financial life. Household accidents, such as pipes bursting, can be costly. As I tell my clients, "Don't expect life not to happen." And as you can see, not all periodics are bad. No one likes to pay for costly emergency plumbing, but we all want to take vacations, and give our loved ones gifts during the holidays.

For the following periodics, write down the amount of money you think you will spend on it for the *entire year*. This will take some guess work on your part. But remember: coming up with any number is better then no number at all.

Car Repair $_____

Even though you may want to assume that your car will never break down, it's quite possible that it might. So if you do not have a new car (which still costs money due to its regular maintenance checks), put down an amount that would cover unexpected car repair for the year. The older the car, the higher the amount should be.

Car Insurance $_____

Many people pay car insurance twice a year. If you do, make sure to put down the annual cost of your car insurance.

Dental $_____

Unfortunately for many, dental costs are a common yearly periodic. If you do not have dental insurance, put down the amount of your yearly cleaning. Even if you do have insurance, most dental insurance only covers half the cost of procedures, and it seems like there is always something that needs to be done, from replacing a filling to an $800 root canal.

Other Health—Glasses, etc. $_____

Health care in general tends to be full of periodics. For example, once a year, I replace my disposable contact lenses. I have many clients who see a naturopath in addition to or in lieu of a general medical doctor. Unfortunately, many of these services are not covered by insurance, and may cost several hundred a year. Are you sure you are taking care of your health? Are you going in for regular preventative checkups? How long has it been since you replaced your glasses?

Season Tickets $_____

Are you a big sports fan who buys season tickets? Or do you go to the ballet regularly? Put down the amount of these tickets. And if you don't go, but would like to, you may want to consider putting down the amount here, to help you see how much you would need to be making to do the things you enjoy. You can always come back and adjust any of these amounts.

Other Entertainment and Hobbies $_____

Some hobbies and entertainments are more expensive then others. I have a client who loves to blow glass, which can be quite an expensive hobby between supplies and renting time in a glass blowing studio. She is more than happy to spend the money on her art that she loves so much. (Your hobby may not be a periodic expense, but a regular monthly expense.)

Kid's Summer Camps/Sports $_____

Parents know that they have to deal with many periodics that always seem to pop up out of nowhere when it comes to kids. Of course, not all can be foreseen. But some can. For example, many parents spend a lot of money in the summer months on extra childcare and summer camps. If your kids are involved with sports, this also brings other periodics. Are there new sport uniforms once a year, and new equipment you always end up buying?

Veterinarian $_____

As with kids, so it is with pets. There is often the unexpected veterinarian bill. While grooming may be a monthly expense, it only takes one trip to the vet to disrupt your finances. Come up with a larger amount the older your pet is.

Vacation $_____

Would you like to take a vacation once a year? Or several mini-vacations? Where would you like to go, and what would you like to do? My husband and I go to the Oregon coast a couple of times each year. We drive, so we don't need airfare, but we stay in lodgings and go out to eat a lot. Every year, we plan for this expense. Even if it has been a long time since you took a vacation, record what it would take to go on one.

Holidays $_____

Countless people suffer from the post holiday "spending hangover," because they overspend during the holidays. What if you had the money and didn't have to either go without, or resort to, credit cards? How much would it take to have a satisfying holiday? Assume you won't go overboard, but also assume you will have money to purchase gifts for those you care about.

Big purchases—Furniture, Computers, etc. $_____

Do you want to buy new living room furniture? Is it time to replace your computer? Has the television gone on the fritz? Do you dream of having a decent stereo?

Other Periodics $_____

What other periodics can you think of? What about property taxes, birthdays, other insurance, yearly health club dues?

Step Two: Decide How Much You Desire to Spend in Your Monthly Categories

Now it is time to decide how much you would like to spend on a monthly basis. Below are categories of expenditures that generally come up every month. Again, you want to think about what would feel like "enough" for you. Can you find a balance where your needs, wants, and savings are all covered? What would this look like? Remember, you can always come back and adjust this. Right now, you are merely trying to figure out how much you would need to earn in order to make "enough." (If you see something that only happens occasionally, add it to your previous list of annual periodic expenses.)

Spiritual and Personal Growth

It's important to take care of ourselves both spiritually and psychologically. This means something different for everyone. How much would you spend *each month* in the following categories?

Donations	$_____
Seminars/workshops	$_____
Church/temple	$_____
Therapy/other forms of personal growth	$_____

Home

Your home is undoubtedly very important to you. And maintaining it requires more than simply the payment of utilities and rent. There is repair work and decorating, and some people have cleaning services. Fill in amounts in the categories that you think would apply to your life if you made enough money:

Rent/mortgage	$_____
Homeowners/renters insurance	$_____
Telephone	$_____
Cell phone	$_____
Gas/oil	$_____
Electric	$_____

Water/sewer	$_____
Cable	$_____
Misc. household supplies	$_____
Plants/flowers/gardening	$_____
Linens/housewares	$_____
Cleaning person	$_____
Other services (such as lawn care)	$_____
Maintenance/repair	$_____
Storage/security	$_____

Food

Good food is an important part of your sense of well-being. But eating is about more than just getting your nutrition. Eating with other people is a primary way that we enjoy each other's company, and maintain relationships, and of course our busy modern lifestyles sometimes require that we eat out. Below, "groceries" means what you bring home from the grocery store. All the other food categories are eating out.

Groceries	$_____
Breakfast (out)	$_____
Lunch (out)	$_____
Dinner (out)	$_____
Fast food/takeout	$_____
Coffee/tea and snacks	$_____

Clothing

Many underearners have clothes that are old, worn out, and out-of-date. Clothes can be an important part of our well-being. When you buy decent clothes and take care dressing, it tells the world that you care about yourself. This does not mean you have to buy expensive and fancy clothes. But do you have enough clothes? Are any of your clothes torn or simply worn out? Some people treat clothes as a periodic expense, as they only shop a few times a year. If that applies to you, simply add it to your previous list of periodic expenses above. Otherwise, think of an amount that would feel good to have each month to improve your wardrobe.

Business clothes	$_____
"Play" clothes	$_____
Shoes/purses	$_____
Accessories (jewelry, belts etc.)	$_____
Dry cleaning	$_____
Alterations/shoe repair	$_____

Self-care

The ways that women take care of themselves vary greatly. What is an indulgence to some, such as a manicure, is a need to another. Again, underearners often don't spend enough money on self-care. If you don't believe you are worth spending money on, then chances are you spend little or no money in these categories. Stretch your imagination and picture what self-care you would enjoy if you had enough.

Toiletries	$_____
Haircut/color/perm	$_____
Massage/body work	$_____
Health Club/exercise/yoga	$_____
Manicure/pedicure	$_____
Skin care/cosmetics	$_____
Waxing	$_____

Healthcare

Ideally, every woman has all her health needs covered. Unfortunately, that is not always true. I've worked with numerous women who were spending money eating out and buying clothes, but were neglecting basic healthcare. Attending to your healthcare goes back to really valuing yourself. Are you worth taking care of? Also, note that some healthcare expenses are periodic, and you may have already covered them when you did your yearly periodic expenditures list (such as contacts).

Insurance	$_____
Medications/prescriptions	$_____
Doctor (MD or naturopath)	$_____
Chiropractor	$_____
Acupuncture/other care	$_____
Vitamins/supplements	$_____

Transportation

Car payment	$_____
Insurance/registration	$_____
Gas	$_____
Maintenance and repairs	$_____
Car wash/detail	$_____
Parking/tolls	$_____
Public transportation	$_____

Entertainment

The ways people entertain themselves are as varied as people are. Some women have many hobbies, others entertain themselves by visiting friends. Use the following categories as a guide. You will probably have to add some of your own.

Movies/video rentals	$_____
Tapes/CDs	$_____
Dating/dancing	$_____
Sporting events	$_____
Magazines/books/newspapers	$_____
Hobbies	$_____
Film/photography	$_____
Parties/holidays/guests	$_____
Cigarettes/alcohol	$_____

Dependent Care

There is no question that kids cost money, but that cost varies tremendously. Some people can't imagine buying used baby furniture, while others depend on the children's consignment shops. School-aged children have very different needs than younger children. There are always costs associated with school, extracurricular activities and the like. If you have children, you will need to personalize this category quite a bit. Also, if you have pets, they are also dependents. At the end of the category are categories for your furry loved ones.

Child care	$_____
Clothes	$_____
Education	$_____
Allowance	$_____
Toys and books	$_____
Health care	$_____
Entertainment	$_____
Sports/extracurricular	$_____

Pet food/supplies $_____

Vet/grooming $_____

Gifts

Some would say that gifts are periodic expenses. I rarely
seem to have a month without a birthday or anniversary. Christmas will be included on your previous periodics list. This category is for birthdays and other occasions.

Birthdays/anniversaries/
   housewarming $_____

Cards/appreciations/hostess $_____

Charitable $_____

Education

If you are in school, you have many monthly costs. There
are many ways to educate yourself besides college. If you are
taking piano lessons, the cost of them would go here. Also, some
people with very involved hobbies that require classes and supplies will list the costs here, instead of in entertainment.

Tuition $_____

Books/supplies $_____

Advancement (such as music
   lessons) $_____

Personal business

This category covers all the personal business in your life.
For example, when I lost my passport and had to pay to replace
it, I listed it in this category. When I needed to renew my grocery warehouse membership, that also fell under personal business. Any time you hire professionals to help you in some
capacity, such as a lawyer or CPA, those expenses would be
considered personal business.

Office supplies	$_____
Postage	$_____
Bank fees	$_____
Professional services	$_____
Internet services	$_____

Insurance

You've already listed insurance such as health insurance and car insurance under their appropriate categories. This is where you would list life insurance, and others.

Long-term care insurance	$_____
Life insurance	$_____

Savings/Investments

Here is where you will put down what you need to have "enough" savings for the future. There are different types of savings for different things. For our purposes, we will look at general savings, for periodic expenses and unexpected occurrences, and savings for investments. Often, investments would be in the form of a 401(k) through your work. Here, put down the amount you could envision investing each month.

General savings (for large ticket items and periodic expenses)	$_____
Investments for retirement	$_____

Now it is time to do some simple math, before we look at taxes. Add up all your periodic expenses for the year from step one. Then add up all your monthly expenses from step two, and multiply this second number by 12 (for 12 months). Lastly, add these two numbers together.

This number is the amount of money you would like to spend in order to have your needs, wants, and savings covered. In a simple world, this would also be the amount of money you would need to earn. However, this is not actually the case. Let's talk about taxes.

Step Three: Calculate Your Gross vs. Net Earnings

Because you pay taxes, the amount of money you earn as your salary or hourly wage is not the same as the amount of money you get to take home. We've all had the experience of looking at our paycheck and saying, *That's all I get? I can't believe how much they took out.* If only we could keep everything we made! But of course then there would be no money for roads, education, and the like. Taxes are a necessary part of life. And remember, the more you are earning, the more you are paying in taxes.

I am not going to get too detailed about taxes. I merely want to give you a general idea of how much money you would need to gross in order to net the amount of money you just came up with. Let's look at a couple of examples. (These examples are based on 2003 tax brackets and assume that you are living in the United States.)

Let's say that when you did steps one and two, the total amount of money you came up with was $50,000. If you had $50,000 to spend and save, you would have "enough." But because of taxes, you have to earn more than $50,000. Now let's assume, for tax purposes, that you are single, on a salary, and you do not own a home. (And my CPA wants me to tell you that let's assume you are not "itemizing.") If you want to have $50,000 available to spend, you would need to "gross" about $68,000. In other words, you would need a salary of $68,000.

Let's look at one more example. Let's assume that when you figured out your periodics and monthly expenses, you felt $100,000 would be "enough." Now let's assume that you are still single, but you own a home and pay about $1,500 a month in mortgage payments. In this scenario, you would actually need to gross about $135,000 a year, in order to net $100,000. To be clear, if you had a salary of $135,000, you would actually "see," after social security and taxes, about $100,000.

Don't worry too much about exact numbers. The point is to remember that you need to inflate your figure to account for taxes. Otherwise, you will still be underearning. If you think $50,000 would be "enough," and you go out and get a job that pays a salary of $50,000, your take home check will be significantly less, and you still won't have enough.

Teresa was fascinated and overwhelmed when she did this exercise. Her annual periodics were about $12,000, and her monthly expenses, after she multiplied them by 12 months, were $38,000. Together, they came to $50,000 ($12,000 + $38,000). Then we added on taxes, and it came to about $68,000.

"Wow, that's a lot! I had no idea."

But when we looked at what she was making, the number was only $8,000 more than what she already made, or an additional $666 a month. When we analyzed it carefully, we saw that making up the difference only meant working about 8 more hours a month (666 divided by $80/hr). Teresa realized that she could make up part of this difference by not bartering, and by not automatically offering everyone a sliding scale. Being clear about what she needed to make made it easier to bill for her full rate. (In Chapter 9, you will see her specific action plan to increase her income.)

The next time Teresa came in, she said she had been looking at various salaried jobs. Some were directly in her field. Others were related to it, such as various positions in human resources.

"I was looking to see who paid what, now that I actually know what I want to be making. If I had one job that paid that, I could let go of my private practice and groups, or I could...."

Her eyes lit up as she considered different scenarios. Once she knew what her bottom line was, she was able to visualize different ways to achieve it. Teresa was coming out of her money fog.

So what is your bottom line? How much would you need to be earning in order to have "enough?" And how would it feel?

What Does It All Mean?

By the time you've calculated what you'll need to earn in order to have "enough," you might feel overwhelmed. Don't. Regardless of how high the amount it is—remember, it's only a number. Think of it as a guide. Just knowing this number will get you closer to it.

Also, it is important to focus first on getting your needs met. If you want, go back through this earning plan and put down only the numbers that represent what you actually need. What is this number then? Once you are aware of your needs and feel confident that you can fulfill them, it will be easier to become more expansive. As time goes on, you can add in other things, such as wants and savings. And it is important to remember that the goal of overcoming underearning is to take better care of yourself. You are worth having enough.

If you are absolutely overwhelmed by this number and do not want to adjust it down, know that you are already on the path to making this amount of money. Overcoming underearning is a process that you've already embarked upon, because you are reading this book. And the next few chapters will give you solid advice on how to go about acquiring this amount of money, from learning how to negotiate, to recognizing and healing the deep disconnect that exists between working and money.

Chapter Seven

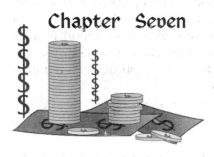

Healing the Disconnect

"What am I going to do? I'm an artist! How can anyone expect an artist to make a lot of money?" Tina burst into tears at our first appointment. She was 38 years old, recently divorced, and the mother of a teenaged son. She had no idea what to do next.

"I've got only two years left until the alimony runs out, and then I'm supposed to be 'self-supporting.' How the heck am I supposed to do that? All I've ever done is art. And I certainly never expected to have to support myself on what I make!"

Tina's anxiety at the prospect of having to support herself was understandable. For nearly 15 years, her husband had provided the bulk of the income for their family. They had met in college, where he was a business major and she was studying textile arts. They were married within a year of meeting, and their son was born shortly thereafter. Tina continued her art, as well as working several interesting jobs, but without a thought of ever trying to make a lot of money. It had never occurred to her that one day she might have to support herself. Besides, she believed that deep down, you couldn't do what you really loved and make money. And she loved art.

"It just isn't fair that our society doesn't pay artists more."
She paused and then added, "I hate having to think about
money!"

Somehow, in her mind, money "defiled" the artistic process. This was reflected in her work history. Time after time,
she had plunged into different jobs and projects with no thought
as to whether she was being paid as much as she deserved. Not
that there hadn't been opportunities to make good money.
During the previous year she was the head coordinator for par-
ticipating artists at a large city festival—a job that could potentially have been quite lucrative.

"How much did you make at that job?"

"Oh, I don't know. They paid me something. I never really
paid attention to it."

"Do you remember talking with them about the money before you took the job?"

"No, not really. To be honest, it never occurred to me."

I didn't bother to ask her if she had tried to negotiate with
them.

Now, in total deprivation mode, Tina was spending almost
no money. She was neglecting herself in several crucial ways,
such as letting her health insurance lapse, and not eating well.
She was terrified that her money would run out, and that she
would be broke. She focused on spending as little money as
possible instead of focusing on how to bring in more.

It's amazing how disconnected work and money have become. In our society, many people work extremely hard, but
remain disconnected from their earnings. It is as if some people
would rather work themselves to death than take the time to
consider money issues. This disconnect is reinforced by our
schools, where money is seldom talked about—it is only the
work you will do to earn the money that is discussed. And the
disconnect goes all the way into our deepest psyches. So many

people are disconnected from what they truly need and want that it is impossible for them to calculate how much they would actually have to earn in order to satisfy those desires.

Recently, I went to a large chain bookstore and stood in front of several shelves of business and career development books. Whatever you might need to know—from how to write your resume to how to decide what to do with your life—was all there. Everything, that is, except how to think about money within the context of your working life. I grabbed a pile of the most promising career/professional development books and sat down to study their indexes, looking for the chapter in each book where money issues would be discussed (such as how to decide how much money you wanted to make, and how much various careers paid). To my great surprise, I found nothing. The closest thing was a chapter on salary negotiation. There was nothing on the financial pros and cons of various fields, and no discussion of the incredibly wide discrepancy in pay between different fields of work.

What did I find? Personality profiles. All the career development books were devoted to helping you analyze your personality and then find a good match with a satisfying career. And, of course, finding a good match is important. You spend far too many hours working to not enjoy what you do. But money is incredibly important as well. After all, it's one of the main reasons that people work in the first place. And yet it is hardly even mentioned, even in books on career and work issues.

Among the better books out there on job change are those in the *What Color is Your Parachute* (Ten Speed Press, 2003), series. This series is about how to do a "life-changing job hunt," and is full of useful and practical information on how to job hunt in real life, using what Richard Nelson Boyles describes as "non-traditional techniques." (For example, he thinks that resumes do very little to help us land the next job.) In the 2003 edition, he lists the nine most common reasons that people pursue a major change in their career. I was fascinated to see that only one had anything to do with money and compensation, given the fact that it is estimated that 50 percent of Americans feel they are underpaid. (This is according to sites such as *workforce.com* and *careerpath.com*.) It seems as though work is rarely related to money, and I believe this "disconnect" has far reaching repercussions for everyone, but especially for women. As you've seen, a lifetime of not earning at one's potential, of not really taking one's earnings seriously or trying to maximize what one can earn in a given position, wreaks havoc on your future financial stability. I can virtually guarantee you that the person you will be in 30 years is going to wish you had paid more attention to these crucial money issues in the present.

As I have previously mentioned, the disconnect between work and money starts even earlier than when we enter the job force. It starts in school, where money is rarely acknowledged or discussed.

Why does no one ask us when we are in school how much money we would like to make? The answer is that it seems like a crass question to many people, so it is rarely, if ever, asked. And a school's silence on making money somehow sanctions one's own natural reticence in bringing up the topic.

While growing up, most girls dream of doing many things, but very few of them consider how much money will be attached to these fantasy occupations. There is still an ingrained sense of reliance on something outside themselves. Women do not have the basic assumption that it will be up to them to take care of both themselves and a family. Therefore, they have the luxury of not thinking about financial issues.

But what if we did think about them? What questions would we ask ourselves? Perhaps we could start by asking how much money we would like to earn someday. Then when we are in school we could ask questions like, *How much money could I expect to make if I study this?* This single question is so important, yet it is almost never asked. Women pay a high price for not asking questions like these. Years later, after decades of low earnings, underearning women will wish they had taken the time to explore these crucial issues.

It is not difficult to find answers to some of these queries. For example, the U.S. Bureau of Labor Statistics cites starting salaries for college graduates. Those graduating with a degree in English can expect to earn $28,438 when they get out. Those who studied computer engineering can expect to make $51,135. That's a difference of more than $22,000 dollars! And both graduates spent the same amount of money on college and invested the same amount of time on their educations.

Please don't misunderstand me. I am not saying to simply pursue what will land you the highest paid job. I believe you have to like what you do. But simply picking the most interesting major, or fascinating field, is not enough. You must take care of your future self by seeking a marriage between doing what you enjoy, and earning decent money. I believe it is possible to find a field of study that will enable you to achieve both. By simply asking the money question, and being conscious of it, you will make more money than someone who has her head in the sand.

And it is more than what you study. People with the same degrees can make wildly different amounts of money because of the ways they consciously pursue their careers. Two women can both study the visual and performing arts, but while one considers becoming an artist after graduation, the other opens a beautiful art gallery.

Peg Cheng, a Seattle-based job coach, shared with me her amazement at people's lack of foresight regarding college and money, and the deep disconnect that exists. "It's amazing how many people haven't thought about their future jobs and the money they will earn, even though they are going to shell out $30,000 to $40,000 for a degree! I see people doing very little research ahead of time on the jobs those degrees get."

I believe that adding a minor in business to any field of study can help a lot. The artist with a minor in business will see many more opportunities than the "pure" artist will. Of course this "pure" artist may look down on the artist who is also aware of finance and business, but the second woman will probably not notice or care, because she will be making enough money to really enjoy life, as well as feeling the satisfaction of using her creativity in her daily work. In contrast, the first woman, the "pure" artist, will think about money constantly, because of the lack of it, and this chronic worry may even inhibit her ability to be creative.

It is also true that the job market has changed. It used to be that a college degree or any kind of advanced training after high school virtually guaranteed a well-paying job. But now, with so many Americans pursuing advanced schooling, the playing field has leveled. Just having a degree doesn't make you special anymore.

Colleges and universities, for their part, have not adjusted to this change. Universities cater to the disconnect between work and money, even though their primary function is to school people for work! The emphasis remains on academics, and not on real world problem solving, and certainly not on future earning potential. This is what is behind the rise of city colleges and vocational schools. They are able to go head-to-head with traditional universities because much of this new schooling is aimed at working adults who are pursuing education with the express purpose of making more money. These schools focus on real world problem solving and excel at helping their graduates land work in their chosen fields. Hopefully, our larger universities will start to think in a similar way, and more importantly, help women to address these important issues.

My husband shared with me a story from a graphic designer he hired that illustrates this problem. She was studying art illustration at a prestigious four-year art college. In one illustration class, the professor began the course by telling the students how important it was to be open to their artistic side, and how much of the course would focus on finding this "inner" artist. She raised her hand and said, "I already *am* open to my artistic side. I've loved art and pursued it my whole life. I'm here to learn the practical skills and applications that I can use in the real world. I'd actually like to find work as an illustrator, so that I can stay in the art world. Will any of that be covered here?" After an awkward silence, the professor finally said, "Well, a little bit, at the end of the course." She then asked, "Do any of the big art schools focus on that?" To which he replied, "No."

Not only do universities not help their graduates think carefully about how much money they would want or need to make after graduation, they also do not give them the skills to market themselves. And of course, most people don't want to focus on these things anyway. The woman who pursues a law degree wants to practice law after she graduates, not worry about where her clients will come from. The young psychotherapist wants to counsel patients, not brainstorm how to build a practice. And for the many who are on a salary, they don't understand the importance of marketing themselves. Being able to "market" yourself in a job setting is very important to raise your visibility and chances for raises and advancement. Needless to say, underearners find this very difficult.

Beliefs About Work

Ideally, women would automatically say, "How can I make money doing this particular work?" or "What would this pay me?" But sadly, most do not. Why do so many people not bother to ask these questions? Because underearners have deeply held beliefs about work and the nature of work and are convinced that it's just not possible to really make good money, so why even try.

This general belief—*It's not possible to make good money*—may stem from our childhood experiences of earning money

in our families and first jobs. Many kids find that it is necessary to perform unpleasant, time-consuming tasks in order to
earn money. You have to scrub the bathtub, empty the garbage, mow the lawn, or do all three. And first jobs outside the
home are little better. Many find that their first job is washing
dishes or doing some other grunt work. It's logical to assume
that all work will be like that.

For underearners, one of the most common beliefs about
work and money is that it is just not possible to make good
money, doing whatever it is they happen to be doing. "*This* job
can't make good money." "You can't really get ahead doing
this." I've heard that come out of the mouth of massage therapists, as well as lawyers, doctors and corporate sales executives.
Whatever their occupation happens to be, underearners are
convinced that it just isn't possible to make good money doing
whatever it is they are doing. And of course with that mind-set,
they are correct. Because they believe their jobs and occupations can't earn good money, they don't earn good money. It's a
natural cause and effect.

Related to this belief about work is the popular belief that
it is not possible to do what you love and get paid well for it.
Some even say that it is not possible to do what you love and
get paid for it at all. If this is true, why can you find people that
genuinely love what they do, and get paid well? The underearner usually says it is due to "luck." But I would assert that
luck has nothing to do with it. If a woman is conscious about
money from the beginning, she can build a meaningful career
that is both satisfying, and well paid. But if she persists in not
thinking about money, and refuses to deal with money, she can't
expect to wake up one day and suddenly earn a good living.
Those that don't think about money issues are usually the same
ones who say you can't make good money doing what you love.

The other dilemma with the belief that it's not possible to
enjoy what you do and make good money is that sometimes
people do end up enjoying what they do, and they may even

find, to their uncomfortable surprise, that they are making good money at it. If they believe that it's not really possible to make good money at something they like, they may avoid accepting payment for their work, or create a situation where they stop making money for the work they enjoy.

For example, several years ago Tina took a position as an art teacher for small children in a local summer program. She absolutely loved the work, the kids, and the hours. It paid reasonably well for a summer job, but Tina would let weeks go by without picking up her paycheck. When the program ran into financial trouble in the middle of the summer, Tina actually offered to be a volunteer, instead of an employee. Not surprisingly, they took her up on the offer.

Another common belief is the assumption that if you made better money, you would have to work harder. But is this assumption true? Does more money equal more work? Ironically, many underearners are extremely hard workers. Some even work more than one job. They can put in long hours for little compensation. On the other hand, most of the well-paid women I know may work during the week, but have their evenings and weekends free. Or they may work intensely for a period of time, and then take the time to relax and play. Most are not workaholics, but have full lives that encompass hobbies, friends, and family.

Barbara Stanny, in her book *Secrets of Six Figure Women*, commented on this erroneous belief, held by many underearners, that women who make really good money are workaholics. What she found, after studying the habits of highly paid women, was actually quite different. "It was the intensity of focus on their work, not the number of hours they spend doing it, that factored so heavily into these women's financial success." In other words, if you work hard during your "work" time, you will free yourself up during your non-work time. I find this to be very true in my own work life. When I am working, I do nothing else. Being self-employed, this can be challenging. But I unplug the home phone, shut the door to my office, and focus intensely on my work. When I am done, I leave my office and shut the door behind me. I believe this compartmentalizing of work and personal time is a key to maintaining balance and a sense of "having a life" outside of work.

Another common belief underearners have about work and money is that there is a "secret" about earning money to which they are not privy. All the people out there making good money must know something they don't. It isn't their fault—they just don't know the secret. Tina said, "My friend Joan makes a lot of money. I don't know what her secret is. She works for this company that does employee training or something. But Joan has always been smart about money. She's just like that."

There is another set of beliefs about work and money that I call "New Age." You've all heard the following phrases: "Do what you love and the money will follow." "Follow your bliss." "Think abundance." The dilemma with these beliefs is that they encourage an abdication of responsibility about money. They say, "Don't worry about that money stuff. Just focus on what makes you happy." And of course we like to be told this, because it's comforting that we don't have to think about money issues. Women are all too ready to believe they can let themselves off the hook when it comes to their finances.

Again, job coach Peg Cheng: "It sounds lovely, and I wish it were true. The premise is good—it's saying that you should focus on using your talents. But often it doesn't work. Being talented doesn't mean you will automatically do well financially. You also have to have business savvy."

I always tell people that instead of saying, "Follow your bliss and the money will follow," say, *How can I make money following my bliss?* The difference between these two questions is huge. It is about trying to balance both money and doing what you love. Remember, it is okay to think about money. It is okay to want money. And it is okay to think about how to get more money. Really.

This is the question that LaDonna started asking: "How can I make money following my bliss?" It forced her to first think about what she would enjoy. With so many years in business, she didn't want to just throw her experience away, yet she was ready to do what *she* wanted to do. She decided she'd like to work with teenage girls and teach them valuable business skills, so that they could create businesses of their own. But how to make money doing this? LaDonna began thinking about contacting potential corporate sponsors to invest in this work, and she also began to brainstorm related products she could develop to sell. Suddenly she was invigorated and enthusiastic about work again.

Perhaps the ultimate disconnect is that women tell themselves that money isn't important. But isn't money the reason so many of us work? Whether women want to work or not, many do so because they need money to live on. Few would disagree with the statement that there are wonderful things we can do with money, so, of course, money is important. Sometimes it is too painful to admit that you don't have enough, so it is easier to say that you don't care about money, or that you are "above" it. And perhaps it's painful to admit that you've never made as much money as you wanted to. But if one doesn't have enough, why isn't the first question, "How can I make more money?"

This goes back to noble poverty. In noble poverty, you can pretend that money just isn't important to you, that you are somehow above it. Remember, if you think that having money is somehow wrong, you will make sure you don't have much. But as we have discussed, many people who are wrapped up in noble poverty actually have low self-esteem and believe they are not worthy of having a lot of money. It is harder to admit this than to claim that they don't want it.

The Deeper Disconnect

When you dig deeper, you see that the disconnect that so many women have between work and money is simply mirroring the disconnect that exists between women and their own needs. Many women are disconnected from what they themselves really need, because deep down they believe that they do not deserve to have their needs, or—God forbid—their wants, taken care of. In fact, many women who underearn do not take good care of themselves. They live in some state of self-deprivation, a self-deprivation that is firmly rooted in low self-esteem.

Eleanor, who worked for the nonprofit, was an example of this. Her apartment was in an unsafe neighborhood, and was itself full of other people's castoffs—old and worn-out furniture. It bothered her so much that she even hesitated to have people over. Her life was full of deprivation, and certainly one deprivation was not having enough money.

Low self-esteem fuels one's self-deprivation—both financially and personally—through continued underearning and by denying one's own needs and desires. So what is the answer? As *Money Demons* (Bantam, 1994), author Susan Forward says in her book, "Nothing is more disempowering to the money demons of deprivation than a shot of self-esteem." But just how does one go about doing that?

In Chapter 2, we looked at self-esteem, and its underlying role in noble poverty. And it is apparent that higher self-esteem is linked to higher earnings, though it is not always evident which one comes first. Does high self esteem lead to higher earnings because you feel better able to take risks and believe in yourself enough to do what you need to do? Probably. But it's also true that when women make good money, their self-esteem also goes up. Inevitably, whether we like it or not, money is linked to our sense of self and self-worth. There is no substitute to being financially self-reliant—to know that you can take care of yourself, no matter what. This sense of self-confidence and self-reliance affects many aspects of our lives.

Believing in yourself and having a good sense of self-esteem does not mean you have no fears or self-doubt. Even women who earn high salaries have fears and feelings of self-doubt when faced with a challenge, a risk, or an experience outside their comfort zone. The crucial difference is that when these women feel fear and self-doubt, they do whatever it is that they fear, anyway. Underearners, in contrast, are usually stopped in their tracks by the fear that they will fail. Further, underearners think in terms of success or failure. Women who are not under-earners do not think in terms of "failures," but rather "setbacks." There is a vast difference. Setbacks are temporary, and can be overcome.

Women can improve their self-esteem by doing two things: taking better care of themselves, and being more aware of their needs and wants. Both of these behaviors can lead to earning more money. The first, good self-care, is crucial to raising self-esteem and feeling that you are worth more money. The second, getting in touch with your needs and wants, makes it almost impossible to persist in your disconnect between work and money. When you know what you need, you naturally focus on earning the money to cover those costs.

Self-Care

Women with low self-esteem become disconnected from themselves at many levels. They lose touch with how to care for themselves, making the unconscious assumption that they don't deserve to be taken care of. And then they assume they are not worth making a lot of money.

One good way to explore self-esteem issues is through therapy, which I wholeheartedly support. In fact, Chapter 9 will discuss how to find an appropriate therapist. But what else can be done? One answer is to start by simply taking better care of yourself. It may sound simple, but for many underearners, it is not an easy task.

Women who have been depriving themselves for a long time become used to a depressed lifestyle. They usually can't remember what came first: they didn't have enough money, so they couldn't afford something? Did they believe that they didn't deserve something, so they made sure they couldn't afford it? Either way, self-care suffers, and this in turn affects our self-esteem. It becomes a vicious cycle.

When Tina and I discussed improving her self-care, she mentioned that she had always thought going to a spa would be fun. But, of course, she immediately came up with a reason as to why she couldn't.

"Of course, I'd love to go to the spa," she said, "but I can't afford it—and it just wouldn't be right to spend my money that way."

We continued to explore the possibilities, looking for what she felt she *could* do. Finally, she agreed to buy herself some luxurious bath salts and new candles, and then treat herself to a long soak in the tub several times a week. Although she had never bought these things for herself, she often gave them as gifts. (Apparently her friends deserved a nice bath!) When I prodded her to think of other ways she could take better care of herself, she conceded that she'd enjoy eating some of her favorite foods—those that she considered too expensive, such as Greek olives and feta cheese. And that was all she could commit to doing.

The change in Tina at her next appointment was truly amazing. When I asked her how she was doing, her reply was immediate.

"Wonderful!" she said, then quickly added, "I still feel a little guilty about doing such nice things for myself, but it sure feels good!"

Self-care and self-esteem go hand-in-hand. As you take better care of yourself, your self-esteem begins to grow. The change takes place subtly, subconsciously, but the result can be powerful. It is as if the mind says, "I guess we do deserve good things. Look at how well she is taking care of us." Keep in mind that this does not have to involve spending a lot of money.

One of my clients who was working on taking better care of herself started bringing fresh flowers from her garden to work every week. The daily color and scent improved her outlook tremendously.

I believe that women who believe they do deserve to take care of themselves naturally tend to make more money, because they see money as a positive force in their lives—one that they can use for better self-care.

✎   **Exercise: Self-Care**   ✎

In your journal, brainstorm three ways you can take better care of yourself. What would feel good, and what would you realistically do? Can you take a bubble bath? Can you give yourself time to relax and enjoy the paper? Can you buy yourself flowers? Write down three self-care activities that you can commit to doing in the next two weeks. Be specific.

Creating a Deprivation Inventory

The disconnect women have between work and money is also due to the fact that many underearners are out of touch with their needs and wants. It may sound odd, but many people don't know what they want and need. And when you don't know all the things you need, and those things you desire, it is difficult to focus on the money you would have to earn in order to cover these expenses. As you've seen, women can deprive themselves of things they feel they don't deserve, and one of the ways they make sure they can justify this deprivation is by not making enough money. After living a life of self-deprivation, these women will lose touch with what they want, and even what they need. I've worked with many underearners who have denied themselves basic necessities, things such as healthcare, dental work, or new shoes. Any kind of luxury is, of course, out of the question.

But the problems that come with being out of touch with one's needs and wants go further than simple deprivation. This disconnect to our needs leads to a disconnect around money— the very money that could satisfy these needs. That is, they may work, and work very hard, but underearners do not connect this work to being compensated fairly for what they do. Because they are out of touch with what they need and want, they do not think of their work as a way to get their needs met. A "deprivation inventory" can act as a catalyst to reconnecting earning money with work.

A "deprivation inventory" is simply a list of your needs and wants. This concept was first developed by Karen McCall, the founder of the Financial Recovery Institute. In her work as a financial counselor, Karen has worked with hundreds of underearners. And almost all of them have been disconnected from their true needs. McCall would ask her clients to compile a list of the things that they truly need and want, and then explore this list with them. Underearners usually resist creating such a list, fearing they will be overwhelmed by such an accounting. Admittedly, because these desires have been suppressed and forgotten for so long, it can feel like they are opening a Pandora's Box.

"What's the point of writing down all the things I already know I can't afford?" one woman asked. "I don't want to think about them."

Remember Eleanor, the woman who worked for the non-profit agency? Not surprisingly, Eleanor had a hard time compiling her deprivation inventory. At first, she only put absolute necessities on it, such as going to the dentist and getting the brakes on her car fixed. But the more she thought about it, the more "wants" she started to add. One "luxury" item she wanted was a new pair of good-quality hiking boots, but because she knew they would cost about $150, she balked at adding them to the list. I encouraged her to add them and eventually she did.

A couple of months later, Eleanor had the opportunity to move into a new position at her work. She was willing to take the new assignment, and, as in past promotions, had not planned to ask for any more money, even though this new position carried more responsibility. But this time things were different. Eleanor had been reading her deprivation list, and she was tired of looking at all those things she couldn't afford—especially that new pair of boots. She got the courage to tell her boss she would accept the new position, but only if it paid at least 15 percent more than her current position. His reply? "Fine."

That was it! Just "fine." Eleanor was shocked at how easy it was. And with her first increased paycheck, she went out and bought those boots.

Because Eleanor had created a deprivation inventory—and kept looking at it—she began to make the connection between her work and her earnings, and her unmet needs, which directly led to her successfully increasing her income.

✎.   **Exercise: Deprivation Inventory**   ✐
Create your deprivation inventory. In your journal make two columns. On the left side, write down "Things I Need;" on the right side, write down "Things I Want." For each column, you will be writing down three things—the date, the item, and the cost. Below is a sample of Eleanor's deprivation list:

What I Need		What I Want	
5/3	New Mattress $350	5/3	New Hiking Boots $150
5/3	Teeth Cleaning $150	6/7	Nice Stationery $25
5/3	Car Tune up $300	6/7	A Weekend at the Spa $400

Keep this deprivation inventory with you and continue adding items to it as they occur to you.

As we've discussed, the disconnect that so many people have with money runs very deep. And at the heart of this disconnect lies the disconnect that many women have from their very needs and wants. When you know what you need, you will more easily be able to connect to your earnings—the very earnings that have the power to satisfy your needs!

Chapter Eight

How to Ask for More

Mary had a resigned look in her eyes. We had gone from talking about her family's mounting credit card debt to the fact that she just wasn't making enough money.

"When was the last time you requested a raise?" I asked her.

"Oh, once, a long time ago. My boss said the company couldn't afford it."

"And how do you feel about what you make now?"

"I guess it's okay. I feel lucky to have a job." She sat in silence for a while, and then admitted, "I was frustrated when they gave Ellen a raise last year. She's only been there for two years. I've been there for six."

Mary proceeded to tell me that she had worked hard for this construction company for many years. She had started off as a secretary and had worked her way up to an office manager, though she had never received more than a cost of living adjustment when she took on the added responsibilities. She watched people around her get promoted, while she quietly did her job, and put in extra hours. It became apparent that her "frustration" over watching other people advance had turned into anger, and a horrible feeling of helplessness.

Why is it so hard for some women to ask for what they are worth? Why do they say nothing and hope for the best?

Why do they take the first no to mean a "no" forever? Because asking for more requires that a woman leave her comfort zone, and it requires that she believes she deserves more than what she's getting.

In this chapter, I am going to give you solid real world skills about how to ask for more money. I've striven to give you practical tools and strategies, and to simplify the process of negotiating and asking for a raise. And I've tried to take some of the fear out of the process. Hopefully, when you fully understand the "game" of negotiation, you will have more confidence to ask for what you are truly worth.

But sometimes simply understanding the process is not enough. Why? Because sometimes beliefs about our own worthiness, or beliefs about what others may think, stop us. "I'd be seen as greedy if I ask for more money." "They might think I am full of myself, that I'm a pushy person, if I ask for a raise." "I should feel lucky to have a job." It seems to be ingrained in us that it is somehow wrong to ask for more. Because when we do, we are putting our own needs front and center. Many women face a lifetime of putting others' needs before themselves.

The "Good Girl Syndrome" often comes into play when a woman considers asking for a raise. *Will they still like me if I ask for more money? Will it make them angry?* We may not think these things consciously, but they usually are not found far below the surface.

Women have been known to sacrifice a lot to keep someone else from feeling uncomfortable. And when a woman fears displeasing someone, she certainly will not stick up for herself adequately in a job setting. In fact, falling prey to the Good Girl Syndrome can keep women from negotiating for their own best interests—be it a salary, a raise, or more benefits. Being a "good girl" can cause women to accept a smaller raise or slower advancement than they deserve. In effect, it causes women to undervalue their services.

Asking for more money, be it a request for a raise or salary negotiation, fundamentally pushes us out of our comfort zone. And no one wants to leave their comfort zone. It's so comfortable! But you've seen the repercussions of not learning how to ask for your worth. When you settle for a lower salary, or don't pursue a promotion, you are hurting your future—a future that you are responsible for. A lifetime of settling, or of being afraid to ask for what you are worth, results in the loss of hundreds of thousands of dollars over your lifetime. And of course it means you have less money right now with which to enjoy life.

The good news is that negotiation is a learnable skill that you can master. Many women have succeeded in asking for their worth, and you can too! To begin with, I'll let you in on a little secret: Financial negotiation is a game. Honest. It's a game that (1) is meant to be played, and (2) has rules. And it is possible to learn the rules of this game. (By the way, an outstanding book on the "rules" and actual how-to of raise and salary negotiation is Jason Rich's *The Unofficial Guide to Earning What You Deserve* [Macmillan, 1999].)

When you take a new job, your new employer *expects* you to negotiate. If you do not, it reveals to him or her that either you do not know your own worth, or that you are incapable of asking for it. This is not a good impression to give anyone. It can in no way help you, and it may encourage others to take advantage of you.

I believe that men naturally tend to see negotiation as a game partly because many men grow up playing sports. When you listen to men talk in a business situation, you will hear many sports phrases. "Well, I guess we lost that one." "Looks like we pulled it out in the bottom of the ninth." "The ball's in their court…" "That was a slam dunk!" This attitude allows them a healthy detachment, and not to take what is happening too personally. I hope that because more women are playing sports growing up, some of this ability to see business situations as a game will rub off.

Many women take negotiating very personally. They view it in terms of acceptance or rejection. Most men do not. I've watched my husband deal with "rejections" in business like water rolling off a duck's back. I've heard him say, "Wow, I'd really play that one differently next time." And then he moves on. I've heard him say, when he was down about a business "loss," "I guess I'll have to fight for it another day." Imagine if women could see negotiating for money as a game—a game to be played. And if we lose, then better luck next time—there is always another game.

On the other hand, women possess many strong interpersonal skills that can make them naturally good negotiators. Women believe in and have the ability to create win-win situations. And in a good negotiation, be it for a raise or settling on a contract, both parties should feel like they've won. You've "won" because you are walking away with the amount of money you desire, and they "win" because they are gaining a valuable employee. Now, in order to create a "win-win" situation, you need to know what they value, and then cater to it. We'll talk about that in a moment.

If you play the game, will it always work? No. Nobody wins every game they play. But if you ask for your worth, you will still end up with more money at the end of the day (retirement) than if you do not consistently try to earn what you are truly worth.

A Few Fundamentals

Before I talk about how to ask for more, I want to give you a few points to always keep in mind. First, you must begin to create a master plan. Ask yourself, *Where does this job fit into my overall career goals?"* If you don't even know what your goals are, it is virtually impossible to reach them. (We'll discuss goal setting more in the last chapter.) You've already calculated how much money you need to earn, in Chapter 6. So how are you going to get there? Will this position lead you in the right direction? Too often, we don't consider a job in the context of our overall career plans, and underearners are notorious for not having career plans. Life just seems to happen, and it is never as good, or as lucrative, as they would like it to be.

Second, never take a dead-end job. Why? Because it is a dead end! Unless it is the perfect job and pays you more than enough, don't do it. Always be able to move upward. And know when you have reached a dead end. A friend of mine held a position as a business manager in a medium-sized company. She had risen to this position over a period of five years. The problem she finally encountered was that the few higher positions were held by young people who had no intention of moving. It looked as if she would stay in her position forever, because the chances of something at a higher level opening seemed slim. She had reached a dead end. So she decided it was time to move to another company. She ended up taking a director level position in another company, and continued her climb upwards.

There are also certain types of jobs that almost always have the danger of being a dead end. Many secretarial and administrative positions can be dead ends, especially if you hold them in a small company. There is often nowhere to move. At least in a larger company, there are times when you might be able to move out of an administrative position.

Sometimes, avoiding a dead end means making a lateral career move, which we will look at under raise negotiation. But always make sure you have possibilities for promotion.

negotiating Your Salary

Although many people know they should negotiate for their salary when they take a new job, many women don't. This is partially because women do not know how to negotiate, and partially because they are extremely uncomfortable at the idea of asking for more. And it is uncomfortable asking for more money, no doubt about it. Most of us were not taught how to do this, and the very idea of asking for more money can give even the most self-confident women butterflies. But if you do not step up to the plate on your own behalf, no one else will. You must be your own best advocate.

The fact that many professional women are uncomfortable with negotiating translates to the notion that they are starting a job with salaries below those of their male colleagues. *This will cost you hundreds of thousands of dollars over the course of your career, because all your future raises are based on where you start!* So it is of paramount importance to enter a job at the highest salary possible. I can guarantee you that most men try to do this.

LaDonna was aware that she was underpaid compared to her male coworkers. Although she had started in similar positions and had similar education to the men she worked with, she suspected that from the very beginning, they had asked for more money than she did. And this had compounded over time. Once, a male colleague she knew from a different company, who held her same position, called her to ask advice on what salary he should shoot for, in a new position he was applying for. When he mentioned what he was currently making, LaDonna was shocked to hear that he made $10,000 more than she did.

I've heard many variations on this story, about women finding out that their coworkers in similar positions make more than them. The most shocking one came from my friend Ana. She was in a high-end sales position with a biotech company and was one of the most competent women I know. She had always made good money and seemed to advance rapidly in her career. I thought of her as one of the few women I knew who was earning at her potential. Yet when I told her I was writing a book on underearning, she shared the following story.

Recently, she had wanted to ask a male coworker a question, and had gone to his office looking for him. This colleague was younger, more inexperienced, and did not bring in nearly as much business as she did. Ana missed him, as he had just left for the day. She was going to leave his office, when she noticed his pay stub lying on his desk. Unable to resist, she picked it up and looked at it, and was dumbfounded to see that he was making almost $30,000 a year more than she was! Thoroughly shocked, this served as a wake-up call for Ana, who had thought herself well-paid. Within the year, she had left the company and went into business for herself, eventually building a million-dollar business.

Remember that women earn more than half a million dollars less than their male counterparts over their careers, and one reason for the disparity is the difference in starting salaries between the two sexes. I am not saying that gender discrimination does not exist. But I do know that women do not negotiate as effectively as men, or as often, and this has a profound effect on their lifetime earnings. I've asked many women what it was like when they negotiated their starting salary or last raise, to find that many women simply have never negotiated. They simply took whatever was offered. Internally, this can translate into, "This must be all that I am worth, if this is what they are offering." But you are worth more!

Regardless of how uncomfortable it is to engage in negotiation, it is an extremely important skill to learn, because the current statistics tell us that the average person goes job hunting in their professional life eight times! So regardless of how much you dislike the thought of negotiating, you must learn how to do it.

Let me say a few things about how negotiable certain positions are. First, the higher a position is, the more negotiable the salary. If you are interviewing for a position in senior management, you better believe they expect you to negotiate! And the negotiation will cover both your salary and your benefits. Lower positions are also negotiable, but not to the degree that higher positions are. You may not be able to negotiate your benefits for those positions, but as you will see, the salary is almost always open to debate, at least to a certain extent.

Second, positions in the corporate world are more negotiable than positions in the nonprofit and public sectors. Often, in those sectors, the pay is pegged to a certain grade, or scale. If you come in at a certain level, the pay rate may be dictated, as it is in governmental positions, or positions within large universities. You may still be able to negotiate for yourself a few extra thousand dollars a year, because even in these situations, there is usually a certain "range" for a given grade or scale. But it is important to remember that what you may need to negotiate is getting put into a higher grade or level, in order to increase your salary.

Now before you begin thinking about negotiating for a particular position, there are a couple of things you must do. First and foremost, you must decide for yourself what your bottom line is. You looked at this in Chapter 6. You must go into a negotiating situation knowing what is the least amount of money you can take, and still be comfortable. Of course, you don't want them to know what your bottom line is! That would be showing your cards. But it is imperative that *you* know what your bottom line is. Otherwise, you risk underearning by taking a job that fundamentally does not pay you enough money. Countless people fall into this trap.

I had a friend who illustrated it this way: She had me take a piece of paper and draw a bull's eye on it in black ink. In the center, she made me write my ideal salary. Then I taped it to the wall. She then handed me a crumpled up piece of paper to throw at the target, but before I did, she turned me around so my back was to the target. So I threw the piece of paper over my shoulder, hoping to hit the mark. Did I hit it? Not even close. "Why did you miss hitting your ideal salary?" she asked. "Because I couldn't see it!" was the response. You have to be able to see your mark if you hope to hit it!

The other way to think about this is to find your "resentment number." Years ago, when I was trying to decide what to charge for an out-of-town talk, I asked Karen McCall, head of the Financial Recovery Institute, for advice. She asked me to think about the amount of money they would have to pay me so that I did not resent doing all the work to get ready, and I didn't resent being away from my husband and (at that time) baby son. "What amount of money would you internally resent working for? If you sit still and really meditate on this, you will know where your resentment number lies. Make absolutely sure you don't go below that number." I thought carefully about this after I hung up the phone and decided what amount of money they would have to pay me in order for me to feel good about going. I called the people who wanted me to speak and proceeded to negotiate with them. I ended up making more than my resentment number had been, and I am sure that if I had not been clear about my bottom line, I would have easily ended up below this number. I would have done the talk and resented all the time away from my family. Instead, I gave a great presentation, enjoyed the experience, and earned good money.

Phase One: Research

There are two phases, or steps, to salary negotiation. The first step involves researching the position. The second step is the actual negotiation. Unfortunately, many people skip the first step. This is a mistake, because doing it is vital to success in the second. Many people walk into negotiation situations "blind," in that they don't know beforehand what the position should pay. This can be disastrous and extremely stressful. So the first step entails researching two different things:

1. What is this job worth?

2. What am I worth?

Believe it or not, it is possible to determine how much a certain position should pay before you talk to your potential future boss. You want to know what the salary range is for a given position. This way, you will know what you can ask for, and you can more evenly evaluate what they offer you. How do you go about doing this? If you are a recent graduate, start with the salary survey information in your college career center. You can also look at job listings which indicate salaries for related positions. Ask your friends and networking contacts what they know about the salary range for a given position. You can call employment agencies or search firms, or you can contact professional associations. Talk to other job seekers to see what they know. And perhaps the easiest and fastest of all: check out the many online salary survey sites. You can start with *www.Jobstar.org* or *www.Salary.com*. There are many salary survey sites on the internet. Simply go to your favorite search engine and type in "salary survey."

Mary spent some time online, researching what similar positions pay with similar companies, and she was chagrined to realize she was working for an amount way below market value. She had suspected she was underpaid, but when she saw in black and white exactly how much she deserved but wasn't getting, her resentment turned to anger. But anger can be an excellent motivating force for taking action, and it was for her.

Notice, by the way, that I've been talking about pay in terms of ranges. It's important to realize that most companies offer a range instead of a set amount, so whoever is interviewing you and hiring you has a certain amount of latitude. For example, a certain position might pay $33,000 to $37,000. The person you are interviewing with probably has the power to give you either $33,000 or $37,000, depending on how qualified they feel you are and how well you negotiate with them. And one of the basic points of salary negotiation is convincing them to put you at the top end of the range. And doing research on the general salary range of a position before you talk to someone puts you in a wonderful position of power. Negotiating blindly is very stressful. How do you know if what they are offering you is more than fair? Or how do you know that what they are offering is actually way below the market standard, and you either need to negotiate them up, or walk away? Researching beforehand is the single best thing you can do to help yourself in an actual negotiation situation. It also cuts down on the stress of being in completely unfamiliar territory.

The second thing that you need to research is what you are worth. After determining what the range is for a certain position, which has nothing to do with you personally, you need to determine what you bring to the table. You will eventually be negotiating with them to put you at the high end of their salary range, or to place you in a certain starting classification. Why should they? What can you do that other people can't? What makes you special? You are going to try to convince them to invest in you over someone else, so you will need to be able to state your case clearly.

Here are questions that you can ask yourself, to help you decide what you are "worth," financially.

- What marketable skills do I bring?

- What relevant education do I have?

- How much experience do I have?

- What are my professional accomplishments and successes?

- What makes me better, different, or more special?

It is important to be able to quantify your achievements whenever possible. For example, "I increased productivity more than 20 percent." Or "I cut down on mistakes in the distribution process by 15 percent." Or "I added more than $200,000 to the company's bottom line." You want to tell them how you can help their company's bottom line, ideally by saving them money or making them money. Anyone can have a hand in this. For example, Mary was proud that she had automated so many office systems, saving her bosses time in processing their orders. Previously, it had taken three days to put a complex order through. Now it took less than one.

As you think about your past experience and accomplishments, keep in mind that it is important to be aware of what skills the potential employer values—skills that may be different than what you expect. For example, a woman may tell the interviewer that she is really proficient in a number of computer programs, only to discover later that it is teamwork and the ability to work with a large number of people that was more important to the interviewer. This can be more difficult to find out when interviewing for a new position. Your friends or people in your network may be able to tell you the types of skills that the company especially values.

✎ Exercise: Let Me Tell You How Great I Am! ✐

Get together with one or more friends who are interested in working on how to negotiate and market themselves. Then play "Let me tell you how great I am!" Take turns telling the friend or group something great about you that an employer would find useful. It could be that you are organized, or that you like working with groups of people. Maybe you have a degree, or you successfully completed a certain project. The object of the game is to go around the circle, each saying one thing, as quickly as you can within a 10-minute time frame. How many rounds can you get in? It will be uncomfortable telling the group all sorts of wonderful things about yourself, but they will be doing it, too. You must be quick, because you only have 10 minutes! (If you play this with more than four people, you may need a longer time limit.)

Phase Two: Negotiate

Now you know the approximate range for the position you are going to interview for, have thought about how to talk about yourself, and know your true bottom line, it's time to negotiate. But before you actually do, make sure they offer you the job first. During the interview your goal is to convince them to hire you. If they bring up money before they offer you the position, say something like "I'm sure we can come to an agreement if you decide to offer me the job."

Also, when it comes time to discuss money, make sure you are talking to the right person. It sounds obvious, but you may psych yourself up to talk about money, only to discover that this person doesn't have the authority to make an offer. If in doubt, simply ask, "Are you the person with whom I negotiate my compensation?"

When negotiating, always be professional. Do not become emotional. This can be difficult at times, but a negotiation situation is not the place to show your emotions, regardless of how angry or excited you may be. Also, never bring in personal reasons why they should pay you a certain amount. The fact that you just bought a house and need to make a certain amount to meet mortgage payments should not come up in conversation. They do not care about your personal issues or problems. At this point, they are trying to determine if you are the right person for the job, and how much you are worth to them.

The basics of negotiation are rather simple (though they can be hard to do). Your job is to make a case as to why they should pay you at the upper end of their scale. You've already made your case for being the best candidate, because they offered you the job. What many people do not realize is that the amount they originally offer you is usually not final. Most people in a position to offer you money give themselves about 20-percent wiggle room. Meaning, if they offer you a certain amount of money, chances are they could increase it by 20 percent if you convince them to do so.

There are two golden rules to salary negotiation. The first golden rule is to never be the first to bring up salaries, if possible. If they've already offered you the job, and haven't talked about money, you can always tell them, "I'm ready to consider your offer." But it's better to wait until they bring it up.

The second golden rule is to always talk in ranges and never in specific numbers. Offering them a specific number is always a no-win situation. For example, if they ask you how much you would like to make, and you can't get them to throw

out a number first, (ideally, you always want them to throw out
the first number), then at least respond with a range, such as "I
was thinking in the $45,000 to $52,000 range." You will know the
approximate range from your research. However, when you give
them a range, always increase it from what you know. If you
discovered that this job pays between $40,000 and $45,000, then
tell them you would like to earn between $45,000 and $48,000.

You always want to stay away from specific numbers in the
beginning. If you feel backed in a corner and end up blurting
out "I'd need to make at least $40,000," one of three things will
happen. It could be that this number is just too high for them,
and they'll feel they can't negotiate with you. Or you could have
thrown out a low number and you'll then be stuck making this
amount. (Sometimes in these instances, they will actually offer
you a little bit more than you said. If this is the case, you know
you were way below what they were willing to pay.) Or you will
happen to hit somewhere in the middle and you'll have to live
with never knowing how much you could have gotten. So never
talk about single specific numbers. Always give yourself room.

The most common "game" of salary negotiation is to try
to get you to give them a number first. They most commonly
do this by asking you how much you made at your previous
job. There is a lot of debate as to how to answer this question,
but believe it or not, you are not actually obliged to answer it
at all. Tell the interviewer that you would prefer to learn more
about the current position before you discuss compensation,
and that you are confident you will be able to reach a mutual
agreement about salary at that time. Or you could tell them,
"I was paid what was appropriate to that position, but this job
is different because…" Even if you do get pressured into telling them how much you made at your last job, always follow it
up immediately with, "…but this job is different. It requires…."

When people ask what you made on your last job, they are
using it as a screening tool. If it is too high or too low, you are
screened out. I asked job coach Peg Cheng what she counsels

her clients on this. She says that if at all possible, do not tell them. It is always an advantage to them, and never an advantage to you.

Still, many people fear this question, and feel they should not evade it. But you are trying to get them to offer up some numbers first. The conversation may go round and round before one or the other of you finally throw a number out. Practice a number of responses before you go into a negotiation. (Shortly, you'll see a sample conversation that deals with this.)

The other common way they go about this is to ask you what your salary requirements are. When they do, evade the question by summarizing the requirements of the position as you understand them, and then ask the interviewer for the normal salary range in her company for that type of position. Again, we'll see this in the sample conversation.

Now let's look at some very specific tricks to use in negotiation. Let's assume that they have offered you the job, and they are now telling you what they will pay. They may give you a range, or throw out a single number. When they tell you the number or range, repeat it thoughtfully, then say, "Hmmm," and be silent for a while. That's it. Do not respond. You want to repeat their offer to them, whatever it is, and then lapse into a thoughtful silence, like you are really thinking about it. I'd recommend you count to 20 in your head, because it is very hard to sit there in silence. The reason for being silent for a while is to give them a chance to offer up more information. Silence is uncomfortable, usually for both parties. They may inject into the silence, "That's as high as we can go!" or "Of course, we are open to discussion." Try not to look excited or disappointed. If they say nothing, then eventually you can say, "Well, it does come near to what I was expecting (if it does) but I was thinking more in the range of…" You will respond with a new range, which places the top of the employer's range into the bottom of your range. For example, if they say something like, "We were thinking of somewhere between $45,000 and

$48,000," you could respond (after the silence) with something like, "I was thinking more in the range of $48,000 to $52,000."

A sample conversation from a salary negotiation follows. Study it carefully and look at all the possible responses you can make to questions. Memorize some of them. If you use only one strategy, you will make more money than if you merely sit passively and accept whatever they offer.

Bill: So what are your salary requirements?

Jane: Well, this is the position as I understand it. *(Describe the position.)* What is the normal range for this type of position?

Bill: I feel we are competitive.

Jane: Great. I'm looking to be paid fairly based on my skills and experience.

Bill: What did you make before?

Jane: Oh, that position had the standard going range for the industry. But this position is different. It requires…*(Name specifics that are up and above your previous job.)*

Bill: Well, that's true. We are looking for someone who can handle all of that.

Jane: Well, let me ask you. Do you see how my skills and experience could be of value in this position?

Bill: Oh yes… So, what do you want to be making?

Jane: Well, I'm open to negotiation. I do like this company, and I feel I can be a real asset here. What is the range for this position?

Bill: Well, the range is from about $42,000 to $48,000.

Jane: $42,000–$48,000? Hmm. (Silence.)

Bill: *(No response.)*

Jane: Well, that's in the ballpark. However, I was thinking more in the range of $48,000 to $52,000, given the level of experience this position requires.

Bill: I think that's going to be too high for us.

Jane: Well, these are my skills. *(Restate them in relationship to what the company values.)*

Bill: That's true, we do need that. But we do have some great benefits.

Jane: Great! Let's settle on salary first. I'm ready to consider your best offer.

Bill: How about $47,000?

Jane: Hmm. Well, because of (this valuable skill), it feels $48,000 would be more appropriate.

Bill: I can offer you $47,500. That's the best I can do.

Jane: Okay, I accept that. Now tell me about your compensation package...

Always have options and alternatives in mind. For example, when a friend of mine was negotiating her salary at a new company, they offered her $46,000 a year. She countered with $50,000. They felt that was too high for them. So she suggested to them that they give her $48,000, and then review her performance in six months. If they liked her work, then they would raise her salary to $50,000. If they didn't, then she would leave. They accepted her suggestion and gave her $48,000. And six months later, she was raised to $50,000.

Remember that one of the primary goals in salary negotiation is to get them to admit your value. And remember that you always have three options. You can walk, accept, or negotiate. I think Barbara Stanny in *Secrets of Six Figure Women* (Harper Collins, 2002), summed it up best when she said, "Asking for more is an act of self-respect. Refusing to settle is a statement of self-worth. And walking away is a sign of self-trust."

Asking For a Raise

Asking for a raise is one of the most feared and awkward things many people can think of, so much so that many simply never ask for one. And in an ideal world, you wouldn't have to. In the ideal world, you would be acknowledged for your work and would be rewarded financially. Shouldn't it be enough that you work hard? Unfortunately, it is not. As uncomfortable and frustrating as it is, you simply must learn when and how to ask for a raise. You risk losing too much if you don't.

Sometimes, it feels as if asking something for ourselves goes against our programming. Women are taught that if they follow the rules and work hard to please those around them, they will be rewarded. This is one of the injustices that is frequently talked about when it comes to fair compensation.

For example, as I mentioned earlier, Mary was frustrated because Ellen was promoted over her. Ellen had come to the company two years ago, and was well liked by many. And it wasn't that she was bad at her job. She was fine. But she made sure that everyone knew what she was doing. Once, she and Mary had worked together on creating a new database to replace their old one. It had taken many weeks. Then a short time later, at a large meeting, a question about the database came up. Ellen quickly spoke up, explaining to the person the intricacies of how to sort the data. Mary sat silently while Ellen basically gave those who were present a tutorial on the database. The impression they came away with was that Ellen had single-handedly created this database. She never said this outright, but because Mary said nothing to correct this untrue impression, many people came away with it. Time and time again, Ellen was able to let the people around her know what she was doing, without being obvious about it. When she went in and asked for a raise, she had many accomplishments to point out, and the boss agreed with her on everything. Mary, on the other hand, did not ask for the raise, and rarely "tooted her own horn." But she worked very hard, waiting for someone to notice her and reward her for her hard work and ingenuity. But of course, no one did.

First of all, how do you know when it is time to ask for a raise? Well, if it has been more than 18-24 months since your last raise, it is time. And if you have been given additional or new responsibilities, it is also time to consider asking for a raise.

When many people think of asking for a raise, they envision going into their boss's office and making a dramatic case for more money, and then crossing their fingers. Actually, most raises are won through organized campaigns, not dramatic sell jobs. And you are more likely to get one if you work within the established evaluation/compensation system of your company. When are raises given out? What is the company policy about evaluations? These are things you need to know. Ideally, you should know them before you even start a job.

When you begin to think about asking for a raise, it is important to think about what standards your boss uses for measuring performance, and concentrate on the achievements they value. As I've said, this is the same for salary negotiation. You always want to cater to what they reward, regardless of whether you agree that it is important. It is easier to discern this when you've been working with a particular boss or company for a while.

Also, think carefully about your evaluations. Many people dread their evaluations, but you should look forward to them. Many companies evaluate their employees once a year or once every six months. Usually, your boss will evaluate your work performance, and you will evaluate yourself, in light of the previous goals you've set for yourself.

Here's a valuable tip: On your work computer, create a file now that says "personal evaluation" and enter into it any accomplishments you can think of. As you accomplish things or reach certain goals, add them to this private list. Otherwise, if you sit down after a year and try to think back on what you have done, you are bound to forget quite a bit. If you keep your accomplishments list updated, when it comes to raise time, you will have much to choose from, and can pick and choose according to what you think your boss would respond to. (And it will be easier to hammer out a new resume, should the need arise.)

Evaluations should not be stressful, because you are filling them out on your own time, and then handing them in. So you should have plenty of time to think about what you want to say. It is one more way to be prepared when it comes time to ask your boss for more money. You should already have a whole list of why you deserve that raise.

Six Steps to a Raise

There are basically six steps to asking for a raise:

1. Be aware of timing.

2. Decide on how much you will ask.

3. Gather all the information you will need to make your case.

4. Set up the meeting.

5. Negotiate with your boss.

6. Be prepared in case it doesn't go your way.

Let's look at these in more detail.

As is usually the case, timing is everything. You should know the company's policy on pay increases, and what its time schedule is. Don't expect to be the exception to the company policy. But if there is no policy set up regarding raises, then it is time to ask for one if it has been 18-24 months since your last one (or since you started), or if you've recently been given new responsibilities.

How much are you going to ask for? Do you want $17 an hour instead of your present $15? Are you seeking a 10 percent increase? Do you want to go from $35,000 to $38,000? You will know what is reasonable from the research you do. (See step one of salary negotiation on page 173 for how and where to research what people make.) You don't want to be seen as having poor judgment by asking too much, but you do want to be seen as a person who knows her own value.

Be armed with information. Make sure you can discuss how you have excelled at your job. Rely on your personal log of achievements. Have you increased profitability or effectiveness? Have you decreased errors? Have any of your suggestions or ideas been implemented? If possible, try to quantify what you have achieved. Make sure you can show several reasons why you deserve a raise.

Now it's time to set up the meeting. Make sure it is with the people responsible for your position. Pick a time that is convenient for them, and make sure you have enough time to discuss your points. You can simply say something like, "Is there a good-time when I can schedule a meeting with you? There are some things I want to talk about," or whatever sounds natural to you. You could also tell them, in a positive, good natured way, that you want to discuss your position and future. "I'd like to talk about my position with you." It depends on how well you know your boss.

During the meeting, lay out your case clearly. You can start by simply saying, "I'd like to discuss my compensation with you. It's been almost two years since it was addressed, and I feel I've accomplished/achieved quite a bit." After you reiterate your achievements with them, ask them if they agree on what you have accomplished.

Mary decided she would ask for a raise, and began preparing. She had done her research on how much other positions paid, and we spent a lot of time going over her accomplishments. She practiced saying them out loud. We did some role-playing, and she practiced different responses. She had also decided that if she did not get a raise, she would begin looking for a new job. She had no intention of telling her boss this, but just knowing it made her feel more confident. Now that she was aware of how underpaid she was, she did not feel as loyal to the company that was obviously undervaluing her work.

She decided she would ask for a 15-percent increase, and she practiced saying this over and over. Finally, she made an appointment with her boss for the following week, and bravely went in, focused on making her case. She carefully explained that she wanted to go over her compensation, in light of her work and accomplishments. She let her boss know that she knew she was underpaid, and used many examples of her successes to back up her request. In the end, although she did not remember everything, or feel that she performed perfectly, she was granted a 12-percent increase. Her boss finally realized that he was in danger of loosing his valuable employee.

Mary was happy with the 12-percent raise. It gave her an enormous sense of accomplishment. She also decided, in this process, that she still might start looking elsewhere in the next year or so.

Your boss may have a lot of power, but many companies have procedures that must be followed when a raise is given out. You may need to allow your boss several weeks to think matters over and set in motion the procedures needed to allow your increase to take effect. You can also ask him or her at the end of the meeting how you can help facilitate the process. Is there something you must do with HR (the Human Resource Department, or personnel)? Is there something you should write up? Make sure you finish any meeting like this by outlining what has been covered and who is responsible for the next step. For example, "Well, to sum up, it sounds like it is possible to get the 10-percent increase, if you can convince the people at higher levels than you. What would you like me to do to facilitate the process? Would you like me to bullet point my achievements so you can go over it with them?"

Be prepared for different responses. For example, they may tell you, "It's not in the budget." Ask them questions about this. Remember, what they are saying may not be completely true. It may simply be a negotiating tactic. Resist thinking to yourself that it is because you don't deserve it. You do deserve a raise!

Ask if a specific amount is allocated to salaries, or a range of dollars. Ask if money can be shifted from one area to another. If your department is cutting costs in one area, could the savings be shifted to your raise? Basically, you are trying to find out how flexible the budget is. Do not be afraid to ask questions. The budget is your business! And your boss will know you are serious. If nothing else, ask whether your request will be considered when they draw up the next budget.

Lastly, you must be prepared with how to react if the meeting doesn't go your way. Maintain your composure and do not get emotional. Make sure you understand your boss's reasoning. Be clear about what you need to do in the future for them to feel you would merit a raise. "So if I understand you, you are saying that once I finish the in-house certification process, you will reconsider my raise?" It is important to outline with your boss what their exact criteria is and specific goals they want to see accomplished, in order to reconsider your request.

It is important that your boss be your advocate. In large companies, where it is easy to get lost, a boss can be a powerful ally. They may need to talk to the people above them on your behalf, and otherwise show real initiative in pursuing a raise for you. And if you are stuck with a bad boss, as unfair and frustrating as that is, you may need to consider moving.

For example, one of my clients had worked in the electronic products department of a large company for about 18 months, when she got a new boss. This new boss was not a good boss, not an advocate for his staff, and it became abundantly clear that he had no intentions of helping the people under him continue to develop their skills and move forward. The natural inclination would be to say, "It's not fair!" And it wasn't. But she had to deal with the situation at hand. So she looked around the company and found a department she thought she would enjoy working in. She made it known to the head of that department how much she would love to work under her, and would be willing to make a lateral move, meaning move without a pay increase. Four months later, a position opened up in this department, and my client was given the opportunity to take the new position, which she jumped on. She received a raise about six months later, and then was promoted within a year. She has continued her climb in the company, while her former coworkers continue to labor under a bad boss.

The company will not always be on your side. Their job is to keep costs down, and yours is to earn what you deserve. The company may have many tactics to keep you from getting a raise. Sometimes they will ask you to wait a year. "We don't have the money now, but if you would only wait until next year, I'm sure we can give you a raise then." Sometimes they try to use the Good Girl Syndrome to their advantage. "The company can't afford it just now, but look at all the other things we offer." "Other people don't make that much…" and, "Don't you love your working environment?" I've had people tell me that the HR department talked them out of a raise because they were told it would put them at the top of their range for that position, and then they "wouldn't have room to advance any more." This is a ridiculous argument. Don't be fooled by what a company says.

If you realize that there is just no way you will be able to move forward in your company, it may be time to move to another company. I realize that no one wants to hear that, but sometimes the only way to continue rising in your career is to leave your company and enter at a higher position with another company. Sometimes, people get "typed" into a certain position, and management just can't see them in a higher place.

Years ago, when I worked for a nonprofit, I started as an administrative assistant. Eventually I worked my way up to a project coordinator. But it felt that I could rise no higher. I saw what the people above me where doing, and wanted to move into their positions. I even had the appropriate education to do so. But they had started with the company at a much higher level. They saw me as an administrative assistant. I was told privately that I would never move up to the places I desired if I stayed. I would have to leave the company, gain experience somewhere else, and then come back and be hired into a senior position. I did want to continue moving up in my career, and I decided to leave. It's possible I could go back now and enter into those higher positions I so coveted, but I no longer care to go back. And I have no doubt that if I had stayed, I would have forever remained in the lower staff positions.

My husband told me about a very motivated and bright co-worker who had an MBA. She was in their marketing department, and worked extremely hard. She was passionate about the company's products, and worked hard to increase their market share. Eventually, a vice president position above her opened, and she applied for it. She was the logical choice, and would have been perfect for the position. But in the end, she was passed over. She had been "typed" into a certain position—marketing—and the higher ups could not think about her in a different capacity. There was also some internal speculation that she was passed over because she was younger and a woman. My husband, who had advocated on her behalf, knew that when she was passed over, she would most likely leave the company, and that is exactly what she did. His company lost a valuable employee, but it was clear to her that she could move up faster if she moved on. A short time later, he heard that she was hired on as a vice president with one of his company's competitors. She took care of herself. And you have to also.

Now What?

You may be feeling overwhelmed with all of this information, but it's important that you have some real-world concrete skills on how to ask for more. Is it hard? Absolutely. But you can do it. Many women ask for their worth, and you can, too. And remember, if you feel shy or overwhelmed with asking for more, there are a number of things to remember that will help you feel better and more in control.

First, remember that all negotiation is based on creating a win-win scenario. When you are asking for more, you are also offering something quite valuable—you! There is no need to set up an adversarial relationship. You both want the company to prosper, and when you feel you are paid your worth, the company can only benefit.

Remember to keep a running log of the achievements and the goals you've attained. Whether you are preparing a new resume, interviewing, negotiating salary, or asking for a raise, being clear about what you've accomplished will also take some of the stress out of the situation. Spend a lot of time rereading what you've written in your log. Practice saying out loud what you have accomplished until you don't have to worry about re-membering what to say. That way, your achievements and expe-rience will always be on the tip of your tongue.

It's best to practice with a friend. It's one thing to look into a mirror and say, "This is why I am worth this much money...." But when you can speak these things out loud to another per-son, you will be that much more capable of saying them under pressure. Practice saying different things in different ways. If you are too embarrassed to list your accomplishments to a friend, use your mother! She may already be your best cheer-leader anyway!

If you consistently try to negotiate a better salary, and you consistently ask for raises over the course of your ca-reer, you will make more money in the long run than if you did not attempt these things. It is in keeping them always in mind that really impacts your bottom line. And remember, this is about more than money. It is also about self-respect and self-esteem. It's about knowing your value, internally, and being able to ask for it in the world. Just keep reminding yourself that you are worth it!

Chapter Nine

Taking Action

In this book, you have endeavored to look at some of the deeper reasons that you act the way that you do around money and earning issues, and how it may be impacting your ability to earn what you need. You have attempted to discover what, exactly, "enough" would look like. You have endeavored to heal the disconnect that has kept you from asking these financial questions in the first place. And you have learned how to ask for what you want.

Now, in our final step, I am going to give you specific actions you can take to tackle the issue of underearning in your life. Remember: Overcoming underearning starts with admitting that there is a problem, and then looking at the reasons behind your behavior. But while a deeper self-understanding is a good thing, knowledge alone will not solve your underearning problem. There comes a point when you must take action, and that is what this chapter is all about. I will give you many possible actions you can take. The more you do, the better your results.

Marketing Yourself

As we've seen, sometimes underearners perpetuate their underearning by failing to market themselves. This is most obvious when one is talking about the self-employed, who need to market their business or service in order to attract clients and customers. But most people are not self-employed, and marketing applies just as much to those on a salary. By marketing, I mean making yourself and your skills highly visible. If your boss or higher-ups do not know who you are and what you do, it will be that much more difficult for you to get a raise or promotion. But marketing oneself can be difficult for underearners, for often they hesitate to stick their necks out. Underearners often live in fear of rejection, and "if you don't put yourself out there, you can't get rejected." Of course you won't go anywhere, either. So you have to begin to think of small ways you can make yourself visible.

How can you make yourself visible? By speaking up. When in meetings, try to think of something you can say that would contribute to the conversation. This may be easier in small meetings. If you have a good idea for something, share it. And make sure you get the credit for it. People often wonder how to do this, but it is not that difficult. If you are walking down the hall and someone begins to talk about a big project you were involved with, you can simply interject somewhere in the conversation, "Yeah, I worked on that project, and boy was it complicated!" If you don't say something, they may not even know you were ever involved.

If you are absolutely terrified of speaking up in meetings, and don't tend to converse with a lot of coworkers, then find other means to make yourself visible. Many introverts have found that they can market themselves in their job setting by writing. Volunteer to write for the company newsletter, or online newsletter. This is a great opportunity to get your name out there, and you can do it in a relatively stress-free way.

Many people market themselves in the job environment by seeking new responsibilities. Volunteer for committee assignments, where you will be working with a group of people—ideally some who have positions higher than yours. Anything you can do to procure a high-visibility assignment will greatly help people notice you, and, of course, will make it that much more likely that the boss will agree with your request for a raise.

There is one other "trick" that you can use: the "priorities trick." Ask your boss to help you set your work priorities. Tell him or her that you are very busy doing various things, more work is coming down the pipeline, and you would like him or her to help you prioritize. Your boss will gladly help you prioritize what you should be doing, and in the process, you will have a chance to show him or her all the different activities you are engaged in. Your boss will then understand the full scope of your work.

Finding a Mentor

How does one find a mentor, and why would one want one? First of all, companies can be complex entities with layers of personalities and politics. Learning your way around this environment in a sensitive way is vital to the success of your career. Unspoken rules dictate who is actually in charge, who really gets things done, how to present something, and when to fight for something and when to let it go. But nowhere will you see these "rules" written down. Finding a mentor can help you understand and navigate this uncertain landscape.

A mentor is simply a more experienced businessperson who can help guide you, and give you advice when you need it. They can open doors for you that regular channels cannot. They can give you faster access to networks and important people. But where does one find someone willing to be a mentor? First of all, remember that many people enjoy helping others. And it is also true that many people feel important when someone seeks out their counsel. Helping someone means you are in a position of power and knowledge.

The other great advantage of having a mentor is that they will often advocate on your behalf. They become invested in your career and truly want to help you move ahead. When it is time for a review and raise, they will often not only give you tips on what to do, but may actually intercede on your behalf.

Look for someone who is in a higher position than you and seems well connected, who knows what you do, and who seems friendly. Then think of some small thing you can ask his or her advice on. You don't want to scare this individual away by asking too much at first. Ideally, find something you can do for him or her. Is there some project you can help with? Can you become involved in a committee he or she is on? The more time you spend with this person, the easier it will be to ask questions. You will be able to see how willing he or she is to help you by how your questions are answered. Start slowly and respectfully. If he or she seems amenable, you may say something like, "I was wondering if I could ask your advice about something." Often, people will begin to feel invested in your career if you seek and then implement their advice.

Kristine, the young architect, definitely needed a mentor. She felt alone in her career and was uncertain how to move ahead. Yes, she had finally decided that she did want to advance, for she realized now that for a long time, her underearning had been serving her. This had come to light when she attempted to get a different job, and had trouble taking action. But now she did want to move ahead, and she began looking at the people around her to see if anyone could possibly offer her guidance.

Kristine was at a loss about how to move ahead, either at her current job or in another, yet she knew there were women who had risen quite high in her field. There was one female senior manager in her office who seemed quite nice, and Kristine decided to approach her for help. First, she looked for opportunities to work with this woman. The opportunity arose when the office landed a large contract for a new office building. This woman headed the project, and Kristine volunteered to join her team. For months they worked together, and they had many conversations during this time, during which Kristine learned things about her company she hadn't known before.

Gradually, Kristine started to ask her for advice more directly. Once, when a group of building contractors they were waiting for was delayed by a couple of hours, Kristine asked her if she could buy her a cup of coffee down the street. During coffee, she asked her "mentor" for more direct advice on how to move ahead in the company. She also asked her advice on whether she should consider leaving and applying elsewhere. Because they were out of the office, they both felt freer to have this conversation. This woman's insights helped immeasurably, giving Kristine things to think about that she had never considered.

Finding a mentor is not as hard as you think, once you look around at all the people in your life. With whom in your life could you talk about your career, on a regular basis? Perhaps this person is someone you work with, and maybe they are in some other area of your life. Chances are that you already know wise people who would gladly support you and give you advice, if only you'd ask.

Networking

As the saying goes, it's not what you know, it's who you know. Networking is about putting yourself out there and forming relationships with the many talented women and men in business. It can be part of your effort to "market" yourself, or be more visible. And often in networking, you meet many wonderful women who may be good mentors.

Networking can be defined as the back and forth, give and take, of business referrals and information. But it is much more than that. Good networking is about relationships, and it is always a two-way street. A good networker networks on other people's behalf, not just her own. A good networker listens for problems and thinks about who she knows that can solve them.

Where should you go to network? There are many wonderful organizations dedicated to women in business. Some are formal, such as Business and Professional Women, a national network with local chapters. (You can read about them in the section Mining the Internet on page 198.) Some vary by city. Seattle, for example, has the "Women's Business Exchange," where women in all types of business can come together once a month for a breakfast, networking opportunities, and a chance to learn a variety of pertinent business information for women. Typically, networking organizations meet once a month, have an opportunity for the members to talk informally with each other, and then host a guest speaker who talks on a variety of business topics for women.

There are general networking organizations, which you can find in the phone book, by asking around, searching on the internet, or perusing the local business publications. But it is particularly important to network within your trade or industry. Most industries host annual conventions and have many networking forums that bring together people in the same field. For example, there is a group called The Association for Women in Communications (AWC) for women in many aspects of the communications and media fields. Reading the publications that are targeted at your specific industry is a key way to find these organizations. What groups to join may be a wonderful question to put to your potential mentor. Tell them you are interested in learning more about the industry and getting involved in more formal networking, and could they recommend any organizations that relate to what you do?

Judy, our events planner, was already well connected, but she realized she did not use her network efficiently for her business. Yes, there were some networking groups she attended occasionally, but in order to generate business, she needed to attend regularly and to get involved at a deeper level. She also needed to attend networking functions with a large corporate crowd, because she needed to be around people who could hire her for their corporate events. One of her networking groups was made up of very small business owners, and these women did not provide the type of connections Judy needed. So Judy decided to join the large chamber of commerce and attend their meetings faithfully, looking for ways to be more involved. She also upped her attendance at the networking functions that seemed to generate the best leads and jobs. Because she was networking more, Judy finally decided to cut back on her volunteering time, because that work was not helping her get ahead financially, as much as she hated to admit it. It was this faithful, carefully targeted networking, that led to the creation of some very lucrative relationships with people in related fields, and people who needed Judy's services.

One final tip about networking: If you find a group you like, attend their meetings regularly. Granted, it can be time-consuming, but for networking to be truly effective, you must do it regularly, or it can be a waste of time. It takes time to meet people and build relationships. A great thing to do is to find a way to be involved at a deeper level. Volunteer to be on a committee. It is at these smaller meetings where you will form relationships. And when all else fails, and you are overwhelmed at the idea of showing up at a networking function and having to talk to people you don't know yet, just remember what Woody Allen said, "Ninety percent of success is just showing up."

Creating a Support Group

A wonderful way to work on underearning is to form with your friends and interested women an "overcoming underearning group." All it takes is a group of women who would like to earn more money.

Teresa decided to form a support group made up entirely of therapists who wanted to stop underearning. Once the group started and word spread, more and more therapists wanted to join. Teresa knew that, like herself, many other therapists had a hard time charging their full rates, and many more did not charge enough in the first place. The group talked a lot about how it felt to charge people for helping them, and how unprepared they had all felt when they went into business. They also talked a lot about money in general, and affirmed how good this felt, because so many of them never discussed financial matters with anyone. It was like shining a spotlight on a dark place in their lives. Of course they all discussed the psychology behind underearning, and the role they themselves played in it. As a group, they supported each other, and helped each other set financial goals. They helped each other maintain the commitment to making more money.

You may want to use this book as a guide, and start your own support group. You might meet once a month, and focus on one chapter of this book at every meeting. You can discuss the chapter, and work on the exercises that are presented in each chapter. You can encourage each other to take action. At the beginning of each meeting, go around and let each member share where she is and what is happening. What has she accomplished since the last meeting? At the end of each group, go around to each person and see if they can commit to one small action that they can do between now and the next meeting. There is no one right way to do it. Simply being around supportive people can go a long way towards breaking the isolation that so many people feel around money issues.

Mining the Internet

We are truly fortunate to live in the age of the Internet. In the privacy of our own homes, we can read and learn about everything under the sun, and that includes career advancement. I want to share with you a number of specific organizations and related Websites that are dedicated to helping women achieve more in business and make more money. Check out these Websites and see which ones feel right for you. Some have online support groups, monthly newsletters, libraries of information, and advice on everything from how to ask for a raise to how to change your career.

Mary spent time on the Internet. At first she studied all the salary guides (and realized she was underpaid). But then she joined some of the online communities as well, and began talking with other women in similar situations. She received a lot of support and encouragement from these women, and even though she never met them face-to-face, felt like she had a true community supporting her in her career advancement.

The American Association of University Women

The American Association of University Women maintains a huge Internet presence and has many resources. From its site, you can also link to many like-minded sites. Its aim is to promote the education and equality for women and girls. It holds national conventions, provides articles and research, and its site contains a very active "member center." The association has more than 1,300 branches. (This may be a great place for you to network!) Its site is *www.aauw.org.*

Advancing Women

Advancing Women, one of my favorite sites, is a great organization that is dedicated to helping women network about workplace issues. It also hosts a large conference each year. The Website contains a career center where you can search jobs and post your resume, and it has many articles in its "workplace" section. Advancing Women also puts out the publication *AW Leadership Journal.* Its site is *www.advancingwomen.com.*

Catalyst

Catalyst is another organization worth checking out. It is an independent research and advisory services organization that works to advance women in business. Catalyst has a dual mission: to enable professional women to achieve their maximum potential, and to help employers capitalize fully on the talents of its female employees. Its site contains a lot of research and publications, and has many articles with great career information. Its site is *www.catalystwomen.org.*

The American Business Women's Association

The American Business Women's Association aims to bring together professional women through leadership, education, networking, support, and national recognition. Its site contains several newsletters you can read, and also has information on educational certificate programs. The association hosts regional conferences, and also put out *Women in Business* magazine. Its site is *www.abwahq.org.*

Business and Professional Women

Business and Professional Women is a great organization dedicated to achieving the equality of all women in the workplace through advocacy, education, and information. It hosts a national conference, and organizes many local groups. Click on "state and local links" to find a group near you. It also publishes *Business Women Magazine.* It can be found at *www.bpwusa.org.*

9to5, National Association of Working Women

The organization 9to5, National Association of Working Women, is an organization made up of working women in the United States, with about 15,000 members. It also has links to local chapters. Its site is *www.9to5.org.*

Women Employed

Women Employed is a member organization dedicated to the economic advancement of women. In addition to a lot of articles and information on the site, it offers "Job Problems Telephone Counseling," a free service. Women Employed also puts out a printed quarterly newsletter called WENEWS. Its site is *www.womenemployed.org.*

national Association for Female Executives

Lastly, there is the National Association for Female Executives (NAFE), which is the largest business women's association in the country, with more than 125,000 members. It offers many resources, including a career center, and hosts a national convention. NAFE also puts out the magazine, *Executive Female*, as a member benefit. It can be found at *www.nafe.com.*

A Word About Time

Before I talk about using professionals and go on to goal-setting, I want to talk for a moment about how you use your time. To start with, I've noticed that many people out of control with their money are also out of control with their time. And for people who struggle with earning issues, time is almost always an issue. Whether you are giving too much time away, or are not organized enough to use your time effectively, time is a huge resource that you must learn to master.

Evaluate your relationship to time. Do you use your time well? Does it seem like there is never enough? Do you feel scattered and pressured? Do you find yourself with chunks of time on your hands with nothing to do? Successful people are good at managing their time. They know it is finite and precious, and manage it accordingly.

But how do you do that? I am a big believer in compartmentalizing time. For example, there are play days and work days. Play days, or rest days, are imperative to have. It's necessary to recharge your battery and have time to enjoy life, without thinking about work or letting it intrude. Otherwise, the time that you do work can be less effective. Make sure when you look at your calendar, you have clearly delineated time chunks. There are times when all you do is focus on your work, and times when all you do is "play."

One way to approach time management is to begin by "mapping" where your current time is actually going. Find a calendar that has each day broken down into hours, and ideally into 15-minute chunks. For one week, simply write down what you are doing at any given time. For example, you called prospects back for 45 minutes, and then had lunch for an hour. Then you filed for 15 minutes and then talked to a coworker for 30 minutes. At the end of the week, it will be interesting to look at your time and see what is actually happening. Is there a more effective way for you to work? Can you look at the week ahead and "map" out your time in a more efficient way?

As we saw in Chapter 7, underearners are notorious for worrying that if they made more money, they would have less time. However, evidence does not bear this out. Many underearners work very long hours, and even have multiple jobs. And when you interview high earning women, as Barbara Stanny did in *Secrets of Six-Figure Women* (Harper Collins, 2002), she found that it was not the amount of hours they worked that lead to their financial success, but rather the intensity of focus they had on their work, when they were actually working.

So think carefully about your relationship to time, and determine if there is something you can do to improve it. There are books on time management, and time management "systems." Take advantage of these resources. Stephen Covey's *The Seven Habits of Highly Effective People* (Simon and Schuster, 1990) is still a great book that covers time management, and his book, *First Things First* (Free Press, 1996), focuses exclusively on time management. Another classic worth reading is Cheryl Richardson's *Take Time for Your Life, A Seven-Step Program for Creating the Life You Want* (Broadway, 1999). When you learn to manage your time, you find that there is enough time to focus on earning good money, and enough time to enjoy your life to the fullest.

Using Professionals

So you want to overcome underearning, but you sense you can't do it on your own? Yes, there are professionals out there to help you, but you must decide what it is you want to work on. As you've read this book, what were your issues? For example, if you feel you are dealing with self-esteem issues, or suspect that underearning is serving you in some capacity that you just can't put your finger on, you may want to consider seeing a therapist. If you want to start job hunting, or need advice on negotiating, you may want to see a job coach. And if you realize you have issues around money, live in a money fog, and are constantly stressed out about your finances, you may want to see a financial counselor. Let's look at each of these professionals in more detail, so you can see if one might be right for you.

Financial Counseling

Financial counseling is a relatively new field that has sprung up in response to the enormous amount of stress and anxiety that so many people feel around money. It aims to help people improve their relationship with money. Typically, financial counselors have a mental health background and work solely on financial issues with clients. Clients often go into financial counseling because they are tired of feeling out of control with money, are tired of living paycheck to paycheck, or long to be free of constant financial anxiety. Typical issues include chronic debt, spending issues, underearning, and couple's communication around money.

"Financial Counseling" can be a fairly general term that describes many professionals who counsel on these issues. (And some professionals call themselves "financial coaches.") However, one organization in particular excels at dealing with people on personal financial issues. The Financial Recovery Institute (*www.financialrecovery.com*) offers "Financial Recovery Counseling" to people who want to work on these issues. Financial

Recovery Counselors aim to help people resolve their issues around money in a safe and supportive environment that is free from shame or guilt. Financial Recovery Counseling is a carefully structured process that helps individuals transform their relationship with money. These counselors are concerned with the "whole person," because they believe that in order to change behaviors, the emotional components of your money have to be addressed. Financial counseling also supplies the tools and teaches the skills needed for effective money management. In essence, they deal with both the emotions behind money and the actual skills needed to manage your day-to-day finances. (If you are interested in working on these issues by yourself, you may also purchase the Complete MoneyMinder System from the Financial Recovery Institute, which includes the *MoneyMinder Financial Recovery Workbook*, forms, and worksheets.)

As a Financial Recovery Counselor myself, I truly believe it to be among the most effective processes available for working on money issues. And of course the stories in this book have come out of my experience as a financial counselor. I've worked with countless women on financial issues, and time and time again, underearning emerges as a core issue.

Regardless of whether you are seeing a financial counselor, or have sought out a Financial Recovery Counselor, it is important to be aware that underearning is only one issue these counselors deal with. Typically, counselors start working with people on spending and debt issues. Remember, a foundation of creating healthy financial behaviors has to be built. However, as you've read, self-defeating financial behaviors, such as chronic debt and general vagueness over money, are big enablers of underearning. It is imperative that underearners stop enabling themselves to underearn. Once the enablers are overcome, it then becomes clear how much money one needs to earn, and the counselors will work with their clients to develop individual action plans to overcome their underearning.

Therapy

I am a firm believer in the usefulness of therapy. Because so many issues we have in life, including money, are rooted in our childhood experiences, it can be extremely helpful to explore these issues with a therapist. Therapists often work on "family of origin" issues, because it is your first family and early experiences that have shaped who you are and given you many, often unconscious, belief systems. Sometimes, these issues are so buried, or painful to deal with, that it is important to elicit the help of a trained therapist to make sense of them. Therapists cover a wide range of issues, from self-esteem, relationship issues, and finding meaning in life, to dealing with sexual abuse, and eating disorders. In terms of underearning, they can be most useful in working with a client on self-esteem. Until a woman truly feels like she deserves to have money, and the good things it can bring her, her underearning will continue unabated.

I strongly encouraged both Tina and Mary to enter into therapy. Tina, the recently divorced artist, had dealt with a lot of deprivation in her life. Even though her self-care had improved in the course of our work, I sensed that her self-esteem could be increased quite a bit. In the wake of the divorce, she was forced to confront a lot of painful issues. And even though she conveyed that she disliked money and what it represented, I knew that deep down, she also felt like she did not deserve to have money and the things money could bring. Mary also suffered from low self-esteem. Given her childhood and unsupportive family, it was no surprise. This had greatly handicapped her because she just did not believe in herself. (Of course, getting the raise gave her self-confidence quite a boost!) Both of these women entered into therapy and gained valuable insights and skills.

As much as I endorse using a therapist, I must add one caveat. Money issues are typically not dealt with in a therapeutic setting. In fact, many therapists themselves are uncomfortable talking about money, which may be due to their own discomfort about charging people for their help. And then again, many therapists are underearners themselves and have difficulty discussing the practical realities of money. Typically, money problems are seen to be merely symptoms of underlying issues that must be dealt with first. Sometimes this is true. But if someone is suffering from a serious "money disorder," such as compulsive spending, then the disorder itself needs to be addressed.

I believe that more and more therapists are recognizing that many money issues, such as chronic debt and overspending, have much in common with the addiction processes. For example, if you use the language of addiction, it is important that a patient stop "using" before he or she can really get help. If not, it is like treating an alcoholic who is still drinking. That is why, in my experience, it is ideal to do both therapy and financial counseling. Each enhances the other and seems to fast-track the process.

In choosing a therapist, it is important to feel comfortable with that person, as well as be certain that he or she is properly trained. In most states, this means they have a master's or Ph.D., in counseling. Many are "marriage and family therapists." Some are MSWs (they have a master's degree in social work), and still others are psychiatric nurses who do a great deal of counseling. However, I believe that even more important than specific training is experience. Find a therapist who is experienced (ideally with more than five years experience in counseling) and with whom you feel comfortable. Ask your friends whom they would recommend, or ask your family doctor. (Sometimes therapy is covered by your health insurance.) Many cities have some form of therapy referral service, often listed in the phone book. These referral services seek to find a match between your personality and issues and the right therapist. Remember, you are hiring them to perform a service. It is okay to ask many questions and to interview them. Also, interview them specifically on how comfortable they are talking about financial issues, and the impact these issues have in your life. Can you talk about money in the course of your work with them? And don't assume that the first therapist you talk with will be the right therapist for you. There are many gifted therapists out there. Take the time to find the right fit for you.

Coaching

Coaching, another relatively new field, may also be useful. Coaching does not concern itself with the past, as does therapy, but rather with the present and future. Coaching is designed to help clients improve their performance and enhance their quality of life, but does not focus directly on relieving psychological pain or treating emotional issues. Many people use coaches to help them stay on track and achieve a desired goal or outcome. Coaches work on all areas of a person's life, and that can include money and job issues. Some coaches focus exclusively on job and career transitions, and are called job coaches. They can also be called a career counselor, career coach, or vocational counselor. It can get very confusing. Regardless, many people will choose one of these professionals if their job just isn't working, if they aren't happy, or if they have a values conflict in their work.

Typically, most job coaches (I'll use that term for now), begin with doing a lot of work on "values clarification"—a search to match what feels satisfying and worthwhile with what you actually do. They will assess your values, skills, personality traits, and goals. Then they will compare these attributes with your current job and the broader market. They will then work with you to create an action plan that will give you the best match.

In choosing a job coach, you want to find someone with whom you feel comfortable. You are also looking for a combination of their credentials, unique skills, and referrals. It can be difficult, because career counseling is not a field with a lot of formal credentials. You can find many good professionals who may not have a lot of formal credentials, but who have a lot of experience. Experience counts for a lot in this field. How familiar are they with the job market? If you go with a job "coach," then they will likely have training and credentials as a professional coach. If you are looking for a coach, a good place to start is with the International Coach Federation (*www.coachfederation.org*). You may also want to check out Coach University (*www.coachinc.com*) and The Academy of Coach Training (*www.coachtraining.com*) to find a coach in your area.

Again, I would add one caveat: Career counselors and job coaches may be very good at talking about values clarification and looking for the right job match, but sometimes they do not discuss money a lot. It is amazing that so many career books do not mention money. So I would be sure to ask them how they deal with issues of negotiation and raises. It's important that they be able to teach you these skills and work with you on them. It's important to never loose sight of the money!

Setting Goals

As I've said before, dreams are just goals with deadlines. So if you've decided that you are tired of earning less than you deserve, and you dream of making more, then you will need to set some goals. It is difficult to get anywhere without setting goals. As humans, we naturally need to have something to strive for, and when it comes to goal setting, the more specific, the better.

Let's look at how one sets goals, and then look specifically at how Teresa, the therapist, set her goals. How does one go about setting goals? The steps are rather simple, but the implementation of them can be difficult. First, you must decide what your goal is. Be specific. Do you want to earn $50,000 a year? I would suggest that you go back to Chapter 6 and see what amount of money you determined felt like "enough" for you, and incorporate that into your goal.

Next, determine what your deadline is. How long will you give yourself to achieve your goal? Then make sure you state your goal in the positive, and incorporate your deadline. "I want to earn $50,000 a year within three years." Do not set a goal focused on the negative, such as "I will stop underearning."

Spend some time creating this goal statement. Make sure your goal is measurable (not, "I'll increase my salary within the next four years," but by how much more, exactly?). And try to create a realistic goal. If your goal is to become an astronaut in the next two years, you may be setting yourself up for failure. (Unless, of course, you already have a Ph.D. in astrophysics or engineering!)

Having a large goal is important, but large goals must be broken down into sub goals, in order to be attainable. You need to feel like you are progressing and achieving. It is these sub goals that will allow you to craft your action plan. You may have a truly inspiring goal statement, but without breaking it down into smaller, more detailed steps, it might be overwhelming. For example, if you want to earn $100,000 in a corporation, you may decide that a sub goal is earning your MBA. This in turn will be broken down into smaller sub goals. Perhaps the immediate goal would then be to research MBA programs in your area and ask them to send you applications.

In working on goal setting, it is important to think about the obstacles that may come your way, because chances are, they will. If you contemplate these obstacles now, and strategize ways to overcome them, you will be better equipped when the time comes. For example, one obstacle that might leap to mind is childcare. How can you attend classes toward an MBA with two small children? Then you would brainstorm out the possibilities. Does the school have on-site childcare? Can family members help? Can you trade childcare with another parent? When people do not think about the obstacles, they often become stuck when one rears it head. They feel like their goal is impossible and immediately become sidetracked. Think now about your obstacles and how you will handle them.

Now that you've identified your goal and begun to break it down into sub goals, it's time to think about accountability and support. Is there someone you can share your goal with, who will help you keep on track? Often, just the act of telling another person what you intend to do goes a long way. Just make sure you choose someone who is supportive and will help you in achieving your goals. (This is where a personal coach can be invaluable, if you do not have people in your life who can fulfill this function. They will keep you accountable and focused. A support group would also be a great way to share your goals with people who can help keep you on track.)

Teresa, the therapist, was ready to set some serious goals. As you will remember from Chapter 6, after Teresa did the exercise of what "enough" would look like to her, she discovered that she would need to gross about $68,000 a year, or approximately $8,000 more than she was currently making. So Teresa set a specific goal: "I want to increase my income by $700 a month by November of next year." This gave her 18 months. She preferred to look at her income on a monthly basis, because she was a small business, and looked at her finances closely at the end of each month. (She learned how to do this in financial counseling.)

Then Teresa decided on the sub goals that she would need to accomplish her larger goal. She came up with three sub goals. Number one was that she would do no more bartering with clients. Number two was that she would try to bring up some of her existing clients who were on a sliding scale, to her full fee. And the third goal was to increase the number of clients she saw each month by five.

The first sub goal of no more bartering did not need to be broken down further. But it was difficult for her. It meant that she needed to let a couple of clients know that she had decided to stop bartering with them. We talked a great deal about this and how to handle it. She liked these people and had bartered for some time. In the end, she decided to just be truthful with them and tell them that after looking at her finances, she decided she should no longer barter. Then she offered to cut her rate temporarily for these people, if they decided that they wanted to continue. She said she would do the reduced rate for six months, at which time her fee would go to the full price. These were difficult conversations for her. One person decided to discontinue counseling, and the other took her up on her offer. Both appreciated her frankness about money. Though it pained her to lose a client, that client had not added to her bottom-line.

The second sub goal, of bringing up some of her clients to her full fee, was also difficult. We practiced what she would say to them. There were two clients whom she did not want to bring up, and she decided that she felt okay about this. It was her way of giving back. But there were four other clients whom she felt should be able to pay her full fee. She realized that when she looked deep within herself, a part of her had begun to resent the work she did with these people. She did great work, and was not being paid what she was worth. So again, she had frank, but sensitive conversations with some of her sliding scale clients. She told them she was reevaluating the way she charged, and was discontinuing her sliding scale. She offered to gradually increase their rate over a six-month period, to her full fee, so they would not feel the impact all at once. Of the four clients she talked with, one decided to discontinue counseling, and the other three agreed to slowly start paying her full fee. Teresa felt good about this outcome, because she was clear within herself that if she continued to charge these particular people a reduced fee, her resentment would only grow.

Her third sub goal, that of increasing the number of clients she saw each month by five people, needed to be broken down further. She decided that this sub goal could be met by doing three things. First, she finally decided to join a premier referral service in her area, a referral service that was hard to get into, but could be a good source of potential clients. Of course this meant an additional time commitment, because this body of therapists met together on a semi-regular basis, but she was willing to make this commitment.

Second, Teresa decided the time had come to buy a cell phone. She had resisted this purchase, but the reality was that if a referral service was going to refer to her, potential clients needed to be able to get a hold of her quickly. Prospects were given the name of three therapists to talk with, and often it was the first therapist who got back to them that they picked. So Teresa bought a cell phone to use in her business.

Lastly, Teresa decided to run an ad in an effort to get new clients. Teresa had long been frustrated with the state of managed care. She felt it was one of her obstacles that she needed to strategize around. Because managed care was spreading, many therapists where not making as much money, because different insurance companies only paid so much for their clients to see a therapist. This amount differed a great deal. So Teresa knew that it was important she increase her number of private pay clients—meaning the clients who paid on a per session basis, and did not use their insurance. Of course therapy costs money, so Teresa decided to run a nice ad in a local magazine targeted at a more well-to-do audience. This demographic had the money to pay a therapist, and was just as in need of therapy as the rest of the world.

Teresa's support group helped her a great deal during this period. They supported her in her action plan and motivated her to continue. There were times when Teresa did not want to undertake a particular action, but because she knew her support group would ask her about it, she found a way to do it. Having a support system is extremely important to keep one focused on one's goals.

So those were the steps that Teresa followed to meet her goal of increasing her income by $700 a month, over the next

18 months. Did she make it? Yes, she did. Because she was so focused on how much she needed to make, and because she had crafted her goal statement well, she was able to stay on track and carry out her plan. She frequently reevaluated her goal and sub goals, and occasionally refocused her strategy to meet her larger goal. Teresa did it, and you can, too.

Looking Into the Future

Take a moment and once again imagine the woman you will be in 30 years. Visualize where this older version of yourself lives and the kind of life she leads. Is she happy? Does she have enough money? Is she living comfortably, and not worrying about her finances? Now imagine that she comes to visit you. She feels lucky to be able to travel backward in time and talk to the person she once was. What would she tell you? Probably many things. The person you are today and what you do now deeply affects her. But one of the most important things that she would tell you would be to take better care of your financial health. How you deal with money now, and the amount of money you make now, deeply affects her. It determines the type of life she can lead, and the possibilities she has. She would probably ask you to pay more attention to money, so she could lead a fuller life, with more opportunities. Can you look her in the eyes and tell her you are doing the best you can to take care of her?

When we underearn, we shortchange ourselves on life and what it has to offer. Underearning means we don't have enough money to pursue our dreams, have the life we want, and a future we look forward to. Underearning, in essence, keeps us from living our lives to the fullest.

It is imperative that we take control of our own lives—we can no longer wait for someone else to do it for us. Waiting for Prince Charming and what he represents is detrimental to our financial health. Persisting in hanging on to old belief systems about the negative aspects of money only serves to hurt us in the future. You, and you alone, are responsible for your life.

Overcoming underearning may feel like lot of work. But in the end, it will be less work than coping with the chaos, and the restricted lifestyles that result from underearning. And remember that overcoming underearning is an ongoing process. For many of us, there is no definite ending. We push through to one level, only to realize that there is another level yet to overcome. Like all forms of personal growth work, progress can feel uneven. At times we seem to make great strides, and at others we feel as if we are not moving at all. But as long as we stay engaged in the process and strive to always be aware of earning issues in our life, we will succeed and go further than we ever thought possible. And we will make more money.

There is no substitute for the self-confidence and security that financial stability provides us. And when we make enough, when we earn at our potential, we feel capable of anything. We can follow our ambition where it leads us and achieve amazing goals. When we earn enough, we know deep down that we can do, or handle, anything that comes our way. There is nothing that compares to the feeling of knowing you can take care of yourself. It means you are fundamentally in charge of your life. And that is what conquering underearning is all about.

Bibliography

Bolles, Richard Nelson. *What Color is Your Parachute?* Berkeley: Ten Speed Press, 2003.

Cameron, Julia and Mark Bryan. *Money Drunk Money Sober.* New York: Ballantine Wellspring, 1992.

Dominguez, Joe and Vicki Robin. *Your Money Or Your Life.* New York: Viking, 1992.

Dowling, Colette. *Maxing Out: Why Women Sabotage Their Financial Security.* New York: Little, Brown and Company, 1998.

Forward, Susan and Craig Buck. *Money Demons.* New York: Bantam, 1994.

Gallen, Ron. *The Money Trap.* New York: Harper Collins, 2002.

McCall, Karen. *MoneyMinder® Financial Recovery Workbook.* San Anselmo: Financial Recovery Press, 2002.

———. *It's Your Money: Achieving Financial Well-Being.* San Francisco: Chronicle Books, 2000.

Mundis, Jerrold. *Earn What You Deserve.* New York: Bantam, 1996.

Orenstein, Peggy. *Schoolgirls: Young Women, Self-Esteem, and the Confidence Gap*. New York: Anchor Books, 2000.

Rich, Jason. *The Unofficial Guide to Earning What You Deserve*. New York: Macmillan, 1999.

Smith, Patricia. *Each Of Us: How Every Woman Can Earn More Money In Corporate America*. Columbus: Q1 Communicators, 1998.

Sorensen, Marilyn. *Breaking the Chain of Low Self-Esteem*. Sherwood, Oregon: Wolf Publishing, 1998.

Stanny, Barbara. *Secrets of Six-Figure Women*. New York: Harper Collins, 2002.

Index

About the Author

As a financial counseling professional in private practice since 1996, Mikelann Valterra has worked with hundreds of individuals, couples, and small businesses to improve their relationship to money in an atmosphere that is free from shame or guilt. She utilizes practical strategies and tools so people can end the cycle of financial chaos. In addition, she addresses the emotional connections we all have to money, so people can better understand their financial behavior.

Based in Seattle, where she lives with her husband and son, Mikelann completed undergraduate work in economics at Fairhaven College (Western Washington University) and later earned a master's degree in Consciousness Studies at John F. Kennedy University. She then studied under financial counseling pioneer Karen McCall, of the Financial Recovery Institute.

In addition to private financial counseling, her passion is in speaking and leading seminars in many aspects of personal finance. Her topics include overcoming underearning, conquering chronic debt, dealing with overspending, couples and money, and exploring the emotional side of finance. Mikelann always operates from the premise that everyone can achieve financial peace of mind.

For information on booking her to present a talk or seminar for your group, please contact her at:

Mikelann Valterra

4509 Interlake Ave. N., #276

Seattle, WA 98103-6782

206.634.0861

Mikelann@mikelannvalterra.comm

Also, please visit her Website, *www.mikelannvalterra.com* for more information, and to sign up for her mailing list.